BEE TORNADO

CHRIS SORENSEN

Harmful Monkey Press / Sparta, NJ

Chris Sorensen — First Edition

ISBN 978-0-9983424-7-4

For JoAnne, Kristin, Pete, and Steve

"If you want to gather honey, don't kick over the beehive."

—Dale Carnegie

ONE

Herc removed his hair band, letting his magnificent mane fall loose. He basked in the warm Colorado sun. Summer had finally arrived, and Herc was here for it.

"Soak it up," he said with a grin.

The sky was a deep blue, the air crisp as an apple. The hogback ridge to the west—referred to by locals as the Devil's Jawbone—stood out in sharp relief against the vivid sky. The rest of the landscape was flat grassland as far as the eye could see, save for a small outcropping of rocks about fifty feet to the south.

Herc's companion busied himself unpacking their spelunking gear from the van, carefully laying out the ropes, harnesses, and other equipment they'd be employing that Thursday morning. Nothing like skipping midweek classes to engage in less academic pursuits.

"Want to give me a hand, Herc?" Benny asked.

"Gimme a sec," Herc replied, stretching his arms out wide as if in prayer, absorbing the rays.

"It'd be nice to get in and out without attracting any attention," Benny said, setting out the kneepads.

Herc shook his head. Benny had always been a worrier. When Herc had provided him with an excellent essay for his American Lit class—AI-generated, of course—the guy had been too chicken to use it, opting instead for a D+. It was Herc's mission to help his roommate learn to chill out. Otherwise, how the heck would Benny ever make it to graduation in one piece?

"Look around, Benny," Herc laughed, spinning in a circle. "Ain't no one for miles. When we ditched the county road, we officially left the grid."

"It's 2023," Benny grumbled. "There's no such thing as leaving the grid."

Herc loped over to Benny and grabbed him by the shoulders. "Dude, do you trust me?"

Benny sighed. "Yeah."

"I didn't hear you!"

"Yes, I trust you."

"Attaboy!"

Herc bolted for the mound of sedimentary rocks jutting from the ground and clambered atop the mound. He picked up a small stone and dropped it into the fissure. The stone hit once...twice on its way downward, but there was no sound of a final impact.

"I dub this grand crevasse...the Devil's Throat!"

"Fantastic," Benny said.

"You may scoff, Benny Shale, you may scoff. But if what's down there is what I *think* is down there, you can say goodbye to working at Starbucks this summer."

Herc knew how much his buddy despised being a barista

—the nagging customers and the dwindling tips. One simple transaction and the two of them could say goodbye to summer jobs and hello to camping, concerts, and cold IPAs.

Herc nudged Benny. "So...?"

"So," Benny grudgingly replied. "If we're going, let's get going."

"Attaboy!" Herc shouted.

———

The temperature in the hole dropped precipitously as Herc rappelled downward, the chill seeping through his nylon coveralls. Most spelunkers typically used a maximum of 150 feet of rope, which they doubled over to accommodate a seventy-foot drop. However, Herc had chosen to use twice that length. Had he been claustrophobic, this journey into the earth would have sent him screaming. The walls seemed to narrow every ten feet or so.

Herc was not a small guy in any sense of the word. He'd been known to down a flatbread pizza and a pitcher of beer after an evening workout. With the harness biting into his belly and thighs, he told himself that it was carrot sticks and hummus from now on.

"How are you feeling?" Benny called. His voice ricocheted about the cavern.

"Like Jonah in the whale," Herc responded from below.

"Like who?" Benny asked.

"Forget it."

Herc's headlamp was doing a good enough job illuminating his general surroundings, but when he trained the beam downward, the depths swallowed the light.

The Devil's Throat, indeed.

He unclipped a Maglite from his belt and switched it on. It lit up the shaft with an unnatural blue-white hue. He aimed the beam downward.

"Okay, I think I see...yup, there is a bottom to this thing." Herc shifted in his harness. "I was starting to think this throat led down to the Devil's Stomach."

No reaction from up above. Herc sighed. He needed some new friends. He was considered a funny guy in Ohio—here in Colorado, well...

Maybe I'm just an acquired taste.

He lowered himself slowly, doing his best to avoid the jerky downward bursts that had been the hallmark of his earliest spelunking efforts. The last thing he needed was to let his impatience override safety. One slipup, and the Devil's Throat would swallow him whole.

As Herc descended, the temperature—which he expected to dip even further—began to rise. He hadn't prepared for that, and by the time he was within ten feet of the rock floor, he'd worked up quite a sweat.

There was something below that wasn't rock—his flash-light picked up a patch of bright, floral colors. Herc's heart raced. He'd been praying for this ever since he had acquired the map. The fellow he'd gotten it from had no idea what he had, and Herc was all too happy to take it off his hands.

Herc made his final descent, dropping to the rock floor below, although calling it a "floor" might not be quite right. The bottom of the shaft was an uneven surface made up of jagged rocks wedged together. He carefully picked his way from stone to stone, feeling like the poor plastic fellow in that game, Don't Break the Ice. If one stone broke free, there was a chance the rest of the "floor" would follow suit.

Herc knelt, mesmerized by the flower that had no business growing in this dark cavern.

"Hello, beautiful."

Besides seeming to thrive in the darkness, the flower was monstrous in size, its leaves larger than Herc's hands. The plant had an odd, prehistoric feel to it. It had a segmented stem and Play-Doh-bright petals. Herc let his fingers play over the iridescent petals, and his hand began to tingle.

Then, the real test...he gave the flower a deep sniff.

His head was suddenly alive with fireflies. A warm, blissful feeling washed over him, causing every cell in his body to sing.

This was it. The prize he'd been seeking.

With weed and shrooms having been domesticated, *this* was the next big thing; he was sure of it. A natural—and *unnatural*—high the likes of which Colorado had never known.

He giggled like a kid and aimed his Maglite upward and let off three short bursts of light—the signal to send down the first duffel bag. A moment later, the bag descended the shaft at the end of a bright, neon rope.

Herc pulled on a pair of gloves and hacked the flower free with his Leatherman tool, which proved more difficult than anticipated. Once he'd stuffed it into the duffel, he hunted around the rocks for its kin. Ten minutes later, he'd found enough plants to fill the first bag.

He gave the duffel's line a couple of tugs, and up it rose, spiraling slowly as it journeyed upward. As soon as it disappeared from sight, his companion lowered a second bag.

Herc spied a cluster of glowing petals hiding between two larger boulders in the crevasse. As he made his way toward them, thanking God for his kneepads as he crawled across one sharp stone after another, he felt the cavern vibrate.

He stopped dead and listened.

Nothing.

He resumed crawling toward the flower.

Herc was mere inches away from the multi-colored blossoms when the ground beneath him gave way.

One moment, he was reaching for the flower; the next, he was dropping into the abyss.

When Herc came to, he didn't have a clue where he was. All he knew was that he was dangling in midair. The darkness was disorienting, and it took a good deal of effort not to panic. His head was pounding, and when he touched his forehead, his gloved hand came away damp with blood.

He gave his headlamp a tap, and it stuttered fitfully, offering him the view in Morse code bursts. What he saw when the lamp chose to work took his breath away.

He was in a cavern below the original shaft. The falling rock must have punched through to this secondary cave. With the scene illuminated, Herc saw that it stretched on forever in all directions—a vast subterranean world.

And sprouting from gaps in the rock floor as far as the eye could see? Enormous beds of luminous flowers.

He felt a series of taps running down the rope. His friend was, no doubt, concerned for his safety. He replied with three steady taps in return. Hopefully, Benny wouldn't freak out and reel him in like a fish. The flowers in this lower section dwarfed the specimens he'd already gathered.

Herc was trying to figure out how to lower himself within reach of the massive crop when a rumbling sound hit his ears. But there was another aspect to the noise—a vibrato that, had it been pitched much higher, might sound like something...

Alive.

Flowers or no, Herc's gut told him it was time to leave.

He prepped his jumar—the device that would propel him upward along the rope—as he steeled himself for the impending ascent.

The terrible sound rescinded like the string section of an orchestra, building to the climax of a horror film soundtrack.

Herc had just managed his first few feet upward when he felt something land on his foot. He craned his neck but couldn't manage the contortions necessary to direct his headlamp toward his boots. He kicked wildly, but whatever the thing was, it held firm.

That was when he felt the buzzing.

His passenger hummed in harmony with the rising noise, and Herc realized that whatever had landed on his foot had company.

He froze. Fear trickled into his brain like venom. He felt the thing crawl up his shin, over his knee...

"There's something down here!" he shouted at the top of his lungs.

At that, white-hot pain erupted in Herc's left thigh as something akin to a steel shaft pierced muscle. He screamed as a burning sensation spread up his thigh, belly, and chest.

An awful metallic taste flooded his mouth, and his throat constricted. He tried to call out again but found his airway was cut off. Soon, he was gasping for air.

The shadows about Herc came to life, swarming over him, hurting him. And as he slipped into darkness, a tune from his childhood buzzed in his head...

I'm bringing home a baby bumblebee,
Won't my mommy be so proud of me,
I'm bringing home a baby bumblebee.
Ouch...!

TWO

"Get us closer!" Derek Stratton shouted down to his driver. The wind whipped his hair as he trained the camera on the glowering sky.

Cheyenne gave the old VW Beetle more gas. Derek was half in/half out of the vehicle, his feet on the passenger seat, sticking up through the sunroof like a tank commander. But instead of chasing soldiers, they were chasing the storm.

The car—the words *Lightning Bug* painted across its side —sped down the dirt road after the line of dark clouds in the distance. By all reports, the conditions were ripe for a twister. The sky was bruised green, and there was an eerie pressure to the air as if someone was messing with the barometer.

Derek raised his camera, framing the shot as best he could despite the bumps and jolts the Beetle threw his way. He spied a particularly promising wall cloud churning away to the south. He nudged Cheyenne's shoulder with his leg.

"Twenty degrees south."

"What?"

"South, south!"

The young woman in the trucker's cap spun the wheel. The VW veered onto a side road, even rougher than the first, and sped off in pursuit.

Derek checked the camera's battery life and was chagrined to find it woefully low. He hated digital recorders, only having recently swapped up from tape. If Super 8 and 16mm cameras weren't such dinosaurs, he figured he'd still be working with film. Derek Stratton was *definitely* old-school.

A section of cloud separated from the rest, curling like the top of a Dairy Queen sundae. This was the moment he'd been waiting for. The storm would either drop a funnel or disperse.

But it was Friday. Derek always felt lucky on Fridays.

He passed his dying camera down to Cheyenne.

"Hand me up the Panasonic."

Cheyenne lifted her head to reply, and her hat went flying out the driver's side window.

"Damn it!" she cried.

Derek was out of time. The clouds were doing their secret dance. Soon, they'd be doing the twist, and he wasn't about to miss out.

He dropped the camera onto the seat and ducked back into the car. He wormed his torso into the back seat, where he searched frantically for the Panasonic amidst the detritus —backpacks, fleece blankets, water bottles, and the odd UFO magazine. Finally, his fingers alighted upon the familiar feel of the old camcorder.

"Gotcha!"

"I lost my hat," Cheyenne complained.

Derek gave the camera a quick once-over. Power? Enough. Tape? Check.

"I've had that hat *forever.*"

Derek sighed. As a looker, Cheyenne was something else; as an intern? Well...

"I'll buy you a new one. Now, get us closer."

"Closer?" the woman asked, warily eyeing the angry sky.

"Closer!"

Derek popped back up into place and removed the camcorder's lens cover. He pressed his eye to the viewfinder and brought the storm into focus.

For a moment, it was just like old times. Him riding atop the *Lightning Bug*, fighting for his balance and some good footage; Molly behind the wheel...

The memory threw him such a curveball that he didn't hear what Cheyenne was saying.

"What's that?" he asked.

"Hold on!"

The VW hit the washboard section of road with a vengeance, the corrugated earth pounding the car's shocks without mercy. Derek felt the front right tire blow before he heard it. Cheyenne slammed on the brakes, doing her best to mitigate the blowout, but the old Beetle couldn't take the strain. A second tire blew. Both passenger and driver braced themselves for the inevitable: the car was going to flip.

But it was a Friday, and Fridays were lucky for Derek.

Instead of tumbling ass over teakettle, the car teetered on two wheels for a moment like a balancing rock before slamming back down on the ground. Derek fell into the passenger seat, the camcorder in his lap. Cheyenne let out a startled cry.

About a half mile ahead of them, the sky split, birthing a dark and angry funnel. It wasn't the finest specimen, but it was there for the picking.

"You okay?" Derek asked.

"No," Cheyenne blubbered.

"You're okay."

Derek was out of the VW in seconds. If he didn't get the shot soon, the whole day's efforts would be for naught.

"Come on, baby. Come on," he begged, as the maelstrom of swirling clouds touched down. Derek planted himself, steadying the camera as best he could. An inner stopwatch started up—if the tornado could just hold it together for two minutes or more, he'd have salable footage. If not...

The funnel began to wobble, subtly at first but growing more erratic. It wasn't kicking up any debris, which meant it was losing steam.

"Hold it together," he urged.

But the twister had other plans. It parted in the middle, the lower section petering out into a weak bluster, the upper section curling back up into the rest of the cloud cover like a cowlick. The show was over. One minute of footage, if that.

Derek lowered the camcorder, released the record button, and watched as the sky swallowed up any evidence of his quarry. He shook his head. Tomorrow was another day.

He turned and headed back to the Beetle. Cheyenne had already extracted her pack from the back seat and was heading back toward town on foot.

"Hey, hold up," Derek called. And when she didn't, he jogged to catch up. "I'll call for a tow."

Cheyenne stopped and turned to face him. She was a

good fifteen years younger than Derek, but her tone of voice made him feel like a little child.

"I'm done."

Derek gawked at her. "Meaning?"

"Meaning I've got better things to do with my summer than chase storms in that clown car of yours. We could have gotten killed."

"What's wrong with my car?"

She adjusted her backpack. "When I signed on, you promised me three things: one, I'd be getting internship credits—"

"You are. You will! Just as soon as I get the paperwork sorted out."

"Two, you'd provide me with room and board."

"I am—"

"A cot and all the mac and cheese I can eat?"

"I lived on ramen all through college."

Cheyenne stared at him, and it felt to Derek like she could see right through him.

"And number three?" he offered.

"You said we'd be doing serious atmospheric research."

He waved frantically in the direction of the now dissipated funnel cloud. "I'd say *that* was pretty serious!"

The young woman nodded, but Derek could tell she'd already made up her mind.

"I hope you catch the big one, I really do. But like I said, this isn't what I signed on for."

With that, she turned and stalked off, leaving Derek and his battered Beetle behind.

***

It was late afternoon by the time Wilson's Towing made it out to the GPS coordinates Derek had sent. Hal Wilson was wary about the offer of a check for payment, but since he'd already made the trek out, he figured what the heck.

"Fifty-dollar charge if your check bounces," he told Derek as his customer climbed into the passenger seat.

Derek assured him it definitely, positively, would *not* bounce and spent the rest of the ride back to Fort Womack wondering how he'd keep that promise.

He kept his eyes open for Cheyenne as they drove, hoping they'd catch up to her, but they didn't. Just like the pitiful twister he'd caught on tape, she was gone with the wind.

"I hate that movie," Hal Wilson snorted.

"Huh?"

"That movie. *Gone with the Wind.* Too long."

Derek realized he'd been speaking his thoughts aloud again. It was a lifetime habit he'd never been able to kick. It always startled him when people around him seemingly turned mind reader.

"Hattie McDaniel won an Oscar for it, I think," Derek said. "Best Supporting Actress."

Hal grumbled and switched on the radio. They rode the rest of the way to the vitriolic ramblings of a political "expert." When they finally arrived at Derek's lot, he was quite ready to part ways with Mr. Wilson and the AM radio personality.

Derek's patch of land was a mile off the main road into town. His neighbors were a defunct gas station and a former flea market. The abandoned nature of the landscape had a definite post-apocalyptic vibe.

The long drive up to the building that served as both

home and business was flanked by sunbaked billboards. *Wild Man of the Rockies!* one touted. *Flying Saucer Debris!* shouted another. Derek averted his gaze as they passed the final sign, but of course, that was the one that caught Hal's eye.

"World Famous Tornado Suit?" he snickered. "If it's so damned famous, how come I ain't never heard anything about it?"

Derek didn't reply.

As they drew closer to the wind-worn metal building, something dashed in front of the truck. It crouched low as it sped past, hairy and four-legged like a dog but with sharp spines sprouting from its back.

"What the heck?" Hal cried, swerving to miss the thing.

"It's just a Chupacabra," Derek said with zero surprise.

"A what?"

The thing zipped past again, and this time Derek could see the wheels beneath the "creature." He'd have to fix that. He couldn't have his little monster giving away his secrets.

"Something from my Odditorium. I guess my daughter's got her out for a joyride." Mel was obviously upset he was coming home late. Again.

Derek spotted his girl sitting on the front steps working the Chupacabra's remote. High above her head was a garish sign. *Stratton's Odditorium*, it read; *Grand Reopening Soon*, it promised. But the museum/money pit looked sad and neglected in the midday sun. Almost as sad and neglected as his only child.

As the tow truck pulled up, the *Lightning Bug* sitting atop the flatbed like a dead cicada, Mel gave her father a little wave. She looked up at the car with indifference as if the broken-down Beetle was just par for the course.

Derek forced a smile. "Chased down a whopper. Just wait 'til you see the footage!"

Mel flashed her own fake smile, and Derek realized he couldn't remember the last time he'd seen her sporting the real deal. Her eyes had lost their sparkle, and there was a heaviness about her no ten-year-old should have to carry. God, if she wasn't growing up to be the spitting image of her mother. His little family—no longer three but two—suddenly felt even more broken than ever.

Hal Wilson parked the truck, and Derek jumped out, holding up the camcorder as if it were prize game he'd brought back to camp.

"Just wait 'til you see it!" he said, doubling down.

Mel sighed and stood. She steered the Chupacabra back to the building and shut it off.

"Show me."

THREE

Mel clicked away at the mouse, setting up the interface between the PC and the old camcorder, while Derek poured them some lemonade. The living quarters of the Odditorium were sparse but homey. Molly had made sure of that. Framed family photos covered the walls, as well as colorful local art. His wife had insisted on clear boundaries between their home and their business, and so, there was no sign of the oddities that lay beyond the apartment's walls.

"I need seventy dollars for my nature club campout."

"Seventy?" Derek asked, leafing through a stack of unpaid bills. "What are you kids planning on cooking out there, filet mignon?"

"It's not just for food. It's for our bug collection. Mr. Armbrister needs it to buy our supplies."

"I'll write you a check tomorrow," he said, setting down Mel's drink.

"What happened to the new camera?" the girl asked as

she tried valiantly to get the computer and camcorder to play nice.

"Ran out of juice. It's not as reliable as the old one."

"And what about *Cheyenne?*" His daughter stretched out the young woman's name, making her feelings for the former intern no secret.

"She's decided to pursue other opportunities," Derek said, pulling up a folding chair and sitting next to Mel.

The girl raised her eyebrows but kept on working. As Derek watched his daughter click open windows on the screen, he noticed a slightly purplish hue to her left cheek.

"How was school?"

"Fine."

"Any trouble on the bus?"

"Nope."

"Because if you had any trouble on the bus—"

Mel turned to face him. Yup, definitely a black eye.

"Do you want to 'play dad,' or do you want to see your video?"

That shut him up. He took a sip of his lemonade and grimaced. More sugar next time. "Playing dad" meant learning a whole lot of new things. Like making lemonade that couldn't pass for furniture polish. And extracting the truth out of a secretive daughter.

Mel hit a key, and the footage popped up on the screen. The contrast was terrible, but that could be fixed. It was the subject of the video that was the problem. They said that the camera puts on ten pounds—that obviously wasn't the case where tornados were concerned.

Derek watched as the twister descended from the top of the screen to the bottom. Almost as quickly as it appeared, it vanished into thin air. If the footage were a fish, he'd have thrown it back.

"That's it?" Mel asked, pausing the camcorder.

"That's it."

"Are you going to try to sell *this* to the Texan?" Her tone of voice told him she didn't think much of the idea.

Derek scooched closer and peered at the screen. "You think you could stretch it out a bit? Make it a little longer? And maybe darken it? Make that purple sky really pop?"

Mel yawned. "Mr. Mix is going to know we messed with it."

"Look, Mel," Derek said, "everybody exaggerates. You're going to learn that as you get older."

"I already know it."

"Come on," he pleaded. "Just a little longer? Can you get it to run two...two and a half minutes?"

"Yeah."

There was that heaviness again, and Derek didn't like it one bit.

Mel hit the rewind button on the video editing software, but the connected camcorder disobeyed, fast-forwarding instead.

"Come on," she huffed.

The day's footage raced forward before video static took its place. Then, without warning, Molly was staring at both of them from the screen.

"You getting my good side?" the woman with the raven-black hair said into the camera.

"Which side is that?" It was Mel, and she was laughing.

Derek choked up. His wife's face and his daughter's laughter—two things that had become so foreign to him.

"Her backside!" Derek heard himself say.

Mel looked up at her father. "Dad?"

The video continued.

"Come on, tell them about the Odditorium," Derek's younger self urged.

"Stratton's Odditorium, opening in three weeks—"

"If the credit card companies don't find us first!"

"Team Stratton?" the little voice behind the camera asked.

"Team Stratton!" Derek and his wife replied.

The couple on screen were about to kiss when Derek reached over and shut the camcorder off.

"You taped over Mom?"

Derek was at a loss for words. "I..."

Mel turned back to the computer. She quickly made a few adjustments to the imported footage and saved it to the desktop before getting up and heading to her room, leaving her lemonade untouched on the desk.

"Hey, kiddo..."

Mel stopped.

"Tapes are...expensive." It was a terrible excuse, and they both knew it. "I mean—"

"I need the check for seventy dollars tomorrow," his daughter said. And then she took off for the seclusion of her bedroom.

Derek thought about going after her. The kid didn't need privacy, she needed a hug. But hugs had been Molly's forte. It wasn't that he was unloving—far from it. But he came from a family of non-huggers, and it had taken his wife to coax the affection out of him.

And now that it's only me, the girl must be starving for it.

He punished himself with a big gulp of the hair-curling

lemonade before jumping on Zoom. But with the slim pickings he had to offer the Texan, he half hoped the man didn't pick up.

No Friday luck this time. Big Jim Mix popped up on the screen, large as life, his Stetson hat perched atop his head. The picture was shaky, and Derek could see meteorological equipment in the background. The man was in the back of a van, and he seemed pissed at being interrupted.

"Make it quick, Stratton. I got an F2 about to take a bite out of Ogallala."

"Listen, I've got fresh footage that would be great for your new show."

Mix's demeanor seemed to soften. "So, you're back up on the horse, huh? Good for you—I admire that. Awful shame about that wife of yours. Broke my heart, hearing about that."

The video garbled as the van hit a large bump in the road.

"Damn it, Weaver! Get your head in the game!" Mix was back. He focused back on Derek. "We got three miles to intercept. Shoot me the clip, pronto."

Derek quickly worked the keyboard and hit send. He waited anxiously as the file wended its way from Colorado to Mix's van. The Texan's phone bleeped and he checked out the message.

"Is this some kind of joke?"

Derek's heart sank.

"Look, Mix—"

"It's bad enough it's one of your weak-ass Colorado twisters," Mix snarled, "but you had to go and mess with the footage. You're wasting my time."

"Jim...I've got bills to pay. I got a kid to feed—"

"Then get me footage of that suit of yours in action," the man in the Stetson snapped. "I'll give you top dollar. Guaranteed. Hell, I'll build a whole show around it."

Derek closed his eyes. "I can't."

"Then we ain't got nothing left to talk about." The Texan turned his attention back to the task at hand. "Weaver! Get the damn lead out!"

And then he was gone.

Derek rose, grabbed the glasses of undrinkable lemonade, and walked to the sink. He poured out the liquid and watched it circle the drain like a little yellow tornado.

He snatched up the stack of bills and sat on the cracked leather sofa, determined to make progress in at least one area of his life, but after tallying up the balances, he set them aside. The business loan he'd taken was just about zeroed out, and the rest of their savings? Ha. Savings were for people who had something to save.

He considered switching on the television and losing himself in someone else's drama, but instead, he replayed his ill-fated conversation with Mix. There was money to be had —the Texan *always* paid for killer footage—but the price to get it was too high. Still...

"Seventy dollars for a campout," he said to the empty room, shaking his head. Seventy dollars for the kid, three hundred to the electric company, three thousand for rent...

Derek stood abruptly. If he went any farther down this road, he'd end up going to a place darker than any storm. No, money wasn't everything, he told himself. He had Mel; he had his business. And in order to help the first, he had to jumpstart the second.

With that in mind, he crossed the room and stood in

front of the door leading into the museum. It had been a good month since he'd last been inside, but it was time. It was well past time.

Derek pulled the latch, turned the doorknob, and stepped into the Odditorium.

FOUR

The large room sat in darkness, unlit and unattended. It was cool as a tomb, and the thought almost made Derek turn around and walk back out the door.

Instead, he flicked a series of light switches on the wall next to him. The overheads sputtered to life, and canned music filled the space—a mysterious ambient soundtrack playing at low volume.

Derek pulled the door closed behind him. He was at the back of the attraction, and when he shut the door, it blended into the mural of the Rocky Mountains that he and Molly had painted on the rear wall.

He moved farther in, taking in the exhibits one by one, revisiting them like old friends. The diorama depicting Alferd (not Alfred) Packer, the Colorado Cannibal, was in disarray. Poor Alferd had fallen headfirst into his cellophane campfire. Derek stepped over the rope divider and righted the mannequin, placing the half-eaten foot back into the dummy's hand.

Next, he visited the UFO display. The flying saucer was

actually made from the salvaged fuselage of a DC-3. Derek had traded the junk dealer box seats to a Rockies game he'd won at the local King Soopers grocery for the privilege of picking through his aviation graveyard. The saucer sat on a dirt landscape with a few tumbleweeds thrown in for good measure. A painted starry sky served as backdrop, and from behind the UFO peered two small aliens. The little green men had been fashioned from two child-sized mannequins from the same auction lot as old Alferd. Their oversized heads were papier-mâché, and Derek could still smell the flour and water mixture Molly concocted to get the strips of newspaper to stick.

Derek found himself getting lost in the world of their creation. He marveled at the Sasquatch Molly had cobbled together out of a Home Depot skeleton and a bunch of Goodwill furs. He laughed at the choir of jackalopes—thirty in all—that sang "Rocky Mountain High" when you pressed a button. And he felt a chill when he passed the Blue Mist exhibit. He'd rigged a fog machine and a small blue spotlight to turn on as one approached the seemingly empty painted mountain landscape. Derek triggered the sensor, and fog rose as his voice whispered from hidden speakers, *"Akin to the Brown Mountain lights of North Carolina, the Blue Mist of the Rockies is a fearful sight few have ever had the misfortune to see..."*

Derek whispered along with the narration, surprised he could remember the clumsy monologue. It was still in his blood, the old Odditorium. Every bit of it.

Save for the last display.

It was last for him, working backward, but first for paying customers. It was the thing most folks came to see.

Fake UFOs and corny dioramas they could get elsewhere, but not this.

There it stood in all its metallic glory: the Tornado Suit. It was one of the few *real* things in the museum, and he'd placed it front and center. *He* had placed it, because by the time the suit was retired, his wife lay in Mount Bennett Cemetery with the rest of her kin.

Derek placed his hand on the suit. It was cold to the touch. He ran his fingers across the chest plate, marking each dent and scratch. The thing was massive, and it had taken tremendous effort piecing it together. Derek never finished college, but the couple of years he put in sparked a love for engineering. A better student could have probably come up with a much sleeker design—his version was as bulky and cumbersome as an old diving suit—but he'd made do with the materials and brains he had on hand.

The suit had a thick helmet with a porthole for peering out at the world. The arms and legs were segmented like a knight's armor. In fact when he wore it, Molly called him Sir Derek the Bold. There were mounts for various cameras, twin oxygen tanks, and a beacon that would strobe when activated. It was beautiful.

It was also the reason his wife was dead.

The display was only half-finished. After getting the suit to stand up straight, Derek had run out of steam. The video monitor to show the famous Tornado Suit in action sat divorced from the DVD player meant to run on a loop. His inner tinkerer saw the dangling wires and felt the need to complete the hookup. After a few quick adjustments, the monitor came to life along with the test footage for the display.

The voice that accompanied the video was Molly's.

"Behold, one of man's most marvelous inventions: the Tornado Suit. Designed by Derek Stratton, this suit was created with the dream in mind to allow bravehearted adventurers the chance to experience the ferocious power of a tornado firsthand."

Derek flinched. Images flashed through his head. Molly helping him on with the suit. The sky turning dark. Wind whipping his wife's hair. Molly screaming...

"Let's take a look at some of this suit's more interesting features, shall we?"

Derek yanked the cord out of the player, and the monitor went silent. He stood there, alone, in front of the great metal beast they'd created, and wept for his wife, for his daughter, and for himself.

He closed up the Odditorium and latched the door. Derek knocked on Mel's door and got a mumbled "goodnight" out of her.

The Beetle wasn't going to fix itself. Luckily for Derek, he was a packrat—he had a number of spares of varying quality in storage. He made quick work of it, and the *Lightning Bug* would live to fight another day.

Wiped out, he tumbled onto the sofa and turned the TV to one of the various history/paranormal channels. It was hours before he was able to sleep. When he finally did, he dreamed of Molly on a mountaintop, spinning around like Julie Andrews in *The Sound of Music*. He knew it was a dream, and yet, he chose to take comfort in it.

FIVE

B ob Kittle was two years from retirement, and he couldn't be happier. He was eager to ditch the trucking life and head on down to Costa Rica, where a little ocean-view cabin and good fishing awaited him.

In the meantime, it was the open road, truck stop food, and long audiobooks. The latter helped keep him going in the wee hours. He'd learned the hard way that music was *not* his friend when driving at night. He'd jackknifed on a patch of black ice between Kearney and North Platte twelve years ago, lulled to sleep by the musical stylings of Perry Como. A month in the hospital and forty thousand pages of paper-work later, he vowed to switch off his radio as soon as the sun went down.

Audiobooks were another matter. Bob had always loved a good yarn, and he figured that as long as he had to put in time behind the wheel, he might as well keep himself enter-tained. And awake. He'd started off renting titles at Cracker Barrels along his routes and was now an avid supporter of

Ears-to-You, a monthly subscription service that kept him well stocked.

He tapped open the app and launched his latest acquisition, hoping for a winner—authors were so hit-and-miss these days. As he passed a sign reading *Fort Womack, 45 Miles,* the story started up, and he settled in for the last leg of the trip.

*"Flatiron Audio presents...*Suckerville *by JD Speers, narrated by Peter Larson..."*

As the story spun out, Bob settled on his game plan: drop the cars he was hauling at the Fort Womack delivery point, grab some fast food, and treat himself to a nice hotel room. Sure, he could park somewhere and spend the night in the cab, but the cramped space had grown a tad musty for his taste, despite his liberal use of air freshener. And he *deserved* a little comfort, didn't he?

Lightning flashed overhead, and Bob groaned. It wasn't raining yet, but it was only a matter of time. There was a turnoff up ahead that could save him twenty minutes getting into town—a county road that veered off from the main highway. He should stick to the main road, but the idea of shaving even a few minutes off the trip was enticing. He'd been driving for forty years, and his give-a-damn had given out after thirty.

He took the exit, winding off and under the highway until soon he was barreling down the alternate route. No annoying billboards for RV dealers, no out-of-state drivers going ten miles under the speed limit.

"...the head flipped over in response, landing on its face. It rose up on rows of teeth and scuttered about like a crab on a hotplate..."

"No, thank you."

Bob switched off the audio. He was more of a Louis L'Amour man. His buddy Walt, who drove long haul for Pickett's Trucking, had recommended the book. Bob made a mental note never to listen to Walt again.

It was amazing how quickly you could put civilization in the rearview mirror. Without sodium lamps lighting the way, he flipped on his brights, flattening out the already flat landscape into a garish white blur.

His phone buzzed, and he glanced over at it.

It was Val, his sometimes/some nights gal-pal. The time was well after three in the morning, and if the old girl was calling, she was on the schnaps again. He considered picking up but only for the briefest of moments. He'd weighed the pleasure of Val's inebriated company against a Big Mac and a big bed, and the latter won, hands down.

The phone blipped—she'd left a message.

Curious, Bob reached out to hit play when something slammed against the windshield so hard, it split the glass from corner to corner.

"Dang it!"

Bob hit the air brakes, and the vehicle stuttered to a halt. He put the truck in park, grabbed a flashlight from the storage bin and hopped down out of the cab. The air was cool, and he wished he'd grabbed his fleece, but he had to make sure his cargo was okay. A rock that size, which it obviously had been, could deflect and hit one of the autos in the carrier and then he'd be up shit creek.

He walked up to the carrier and clicked on the light.

"Slap me sideways..."

As he ran the flashlight beam the length of the

truck, his eyes went wide. Almost every single one of the cars he was hauling had their windshields bashed in.

"Dang it," he repeated, his mouth going dry.

A streak of lightning overhead illuminated the scene, and Bob could swear that the cars were moving. Not back and forth—they were secured to the carrier—but undulating like they were covered in ants or...

A low buzz rose from the cars, and Bob just about dropped the flashlight. He slowly backed away as thunder rolled. He needed to get back in the cab. *Now.*

Bob tried to keep control of his nerves, but by the time he'd crawled back into the cab and locked the door, his teeth were actually chattering. He fumbled at his CB, and the air filled with overlapping voices.

"Breaker 1-9, this is Heart Attack," Bob stammered. "Me and my portable parking lot's out here on Old Damascus Road, four miles east of Fort Womack. I got me a 10-200, people."

As he spoke, something crawled onto the windshield from the top of his cab. It was the size of a rat, but it was no rat—Bob recognized its shape instantly.

But it's too big, he thought.

It was a bee. And it was followed by another and another. And when the lightning flashed again, he saw that the entire cab was engulfed.

"Anyone got their ears on? I repeat: I got a 10-200. A big, *big* 10-200."

The CB crackled as another monster bolt lit up the night. He got no reply. He was on his own.

"Get to town," Bob told himself, forcing his hand onto

the gear shift. "Get her up to speed, let the wind do the rest. Get to town, Bob."

Before he could make another move, an enormous stinger plunged through the driver's side window. Venom dripped from its tip. Two more pierced the window on the passenger's side. Clawed feet up worked their way inside through cracks in the glass.

When the windows shattered, and the bees flooded in, all Bob could think about was a cold beer and the turquoise sea stretching out as far as the eye could see.

SIX

The jarring sound of a buzzer woke Derek with a start. He sat up, unsure for a moment where he was.

I slept on the sofa, not in bed.

The TV was still on. And on the screen was none other than Big Jim Mix himself. The man was decked out in full safari gear—a ridiculous outfit but one that probably played well with his audience.

"Next time, on Big Jim Mix's Worlds of Wonder!"

The screen flashed to a clip of Mix sitting with a group of people eating stew. He flashed a thumbs-up.

"I chew the fat with the cannibals of New Guinea..."

The scene shifted to Mix chasing a glowing figure through a cemetery with a revolver.

"I bring the ghost of Lee Harvey Oswald to justice..."

Last but not least, a rapid edit of a handful of monstrous tornados eating up the landscape.

"And as always, I present you with the best in tornados, tornados, tornados!"

Derek snorted and switched off the TV.

The buzzer rang a second time.

"No one's home!" he called. What time was it?

He rose, his back barking on account of the sofa's broken springs. He twisted, hearing his spine pop. He wasn't sure if bill collectors made house calls, but if they did, he was in no mood to chat.

"Go away."

His visitor rapped loudly on the door, abandoning the buzzer. Whoever had come to call was nothing if not persistent.

Derek shuffled toward the door, noting the time on the microwave: 10:16. To say he'd slept in was an understatement. Where was Mel? Surely she wasn't still in bed. It was Saturday morning, and she tended to be wound up on weekends. Crunching her cereal, demanding the use of the TV. Was it possible they'd *both* slept in?

He was just about to the door when the person on the other side made her presence known.

"Derek! It's Shelby. Open up."

Shelby? What did she want? He hadn't seen her in months. Not that he'd exactly put out the welcome mat.

He pulled open the door and shielded his eyes from the sun's glare. Shelby stood before him in her crisp blue uniform and sunglasses that hid her mood quite well. Waking up to a cop on your doorstep was one thing; waking up to your dead wife's sister was another.

"Late night?" Shelby asked. She was shorter than Molly had been. More compact. But she had the same jet-black hair and Parker family nose he knew so well.

"You could say that," Derek said. It was then that he noticed that Shelby wasn't alone. Mel was peering at him from behind the woman in blue, her backpack over her shoulders. "What's going on?"

"Do you want the good news first or the bad news?"

Derek pinched the bridge of his nose. As lucky as Fridays were for him, Saturdays tended to swing the other way.

"What the heck...give me the good first," he said.

"Your daughter was just caught trying to cash a bad check."

She handed the check in question over to Derek. He took one look at it and winced. Seventy dollars, made out to cash with a child's scrawl for a signature.

He locked eyes with Mel. "What were you thinking?"

Shelby held out a hand, calming Derek. "Luckily, I was able to sweep it under the rug. But she can't visit the Butte Bank again. Ever."

"Mel," Derek sighed.

The girl looked at her shoes. "I told you I needed it today."

Guilt washed over him, but he knew he hadn't heard everything Shelby had to say.

"If *this* is the good news, what's the bad?"

Shelby serpentined through the crowd, driving slowly down Fort Womack's main thoroughfare, setting off the cruiser's *bleep* every time revelers got in her way. Banners announcing the Fourth Annual ShakesBeer Festival adorned the majority of the town's brick storefronts, and flags touting local breweries' Bard-themed beers waved in the breeze. Sir Toby Stout, Out Damn Spot Red, Aguecheek Pale Ale. The list went on and on.

"What genius came up with the ShakesBeer Festival anyway?" she complained. "It's just another excuse for day drinking, if you ask me."

She laid on the horn as a young man in a jester's outfit toting a plastic yard of ale stumbled in the cruiser's path. The man nearly tripped, righted himself, and ended with an overly dramatic bow, spilling a good deal of beer in the process.

"See what I mean?"

Derek shifted in the passenger seat. At least his sister-in-law let him sit up front. Mel was happy to be in the back. She'd been a whirlwind of questions when they first headed out. Had Shelby ever transported a murderer? Had anyone ever tried to escape? Had anybody ever thrown up in the back seat? Mel seemed pleased when the answer to each question came back "yes." Derek noticed a definite change in his daughter—Shelby brought out a brightness in her. Maybe it was the result of boredom hanging around just him day in and day out. Maybe she needed a female presence in her life. Or maybe the kid just liked talking about the nuts and bolts—and blood and guts—of police work.

"Do you mind telling me where we're going?" he asked.

"Yes," Shelby said.

The woman adjusted her rearview mirror to get a better look at her niece. The girl was sorting through her backpack. Mel retrieved her sunglasses and put them on, imitating her aunt.

"How are you liking your nature group?"

"It's okay. It's kind of weird being the only girl, but all those other groups do is sell cookies."

"I hear you, kid," Shelby said. "There was a time I was the only woman on the Fort Womack PD. There's a bunch of us now, but back then? Not exactly what I'd call fun. Tell me—what did you need the money for?"

The question caught Mel off guard, and Derek realized that she must have been tightlipped about it ever since getting sprung. Now, she answered directly and without guile.

"We're going on an overnight bug hunt. And Dad didn't give me the money to go."

"Hey," Derek interjected. "That's private, family business."

"Aunt Shelby's family."

"Don't worry, kid," Shelby said, driving around a seven-seat conference bike ridden by what appeared to be the entire cast of *Midsummer Night's Dream*, complete with a man wearing a rubber donkey head. "I'll spot you."

This rubbed Derek the wrong way. Actually, it pissed him off.

"You'll spot her? I guess that makes me the *bad* cop."

"If the shoe fits..."

"What does that mean?"

Shelby scowled. "Let's not do this in front of the kid."

"You think I'm the reason she tried to pass that check."

"No, Derek, that was her choice and a bad one at that. I just think you dropped the ball, that's all."

"Dropped the ball?"

"Like you always do," Shelby finished under her breath.

"Like I did with Molly?"

Shelby hit the brakes. An elderly woman with snow-white hair and a walker crossed ever so slowly in front of the car. Her faerie outfit left little to the imagination.

Shelby spoke low, making sure only Derek could hear. "Mention my dead sister again, and I'm putting you in cuffs, capisce?"

With that, she zipped around the woman with the walker, causing her little outfit to flutter. Shelby didn't say another word for the rest of the drive.

The drive took them south through town and out onto the prairie, the still-snowcapped mountains to the west.

Derek had hoped Shelby would fill him in on the way to wherever she was taking them, but that was not to be. He didn't press, however—she'd turned a blind eye to his daughter's felonious ways, and so he was obliged to go along for the ride. But when they got off the main route and jumped onto a side road, abandoning pavement for dirt, he couldn't keep silent anymore.

"Look, I enjoy a nice drive as much as anyone, but don't you think it's about time to clue me in? Or are you going to wait until we hit Albuquerque?"

"We're here," Shelby replied.

She slowed the cruiser and pulled it over to the side of the road. A green van sat parked amidst a patch of scrub grass, roped off by crime scene tape. Its owners were nowhere to be seen.

Shelby put the car in park and shut it off. She turned to Derek.

"Come on."

"How can I resist?"

Mel popped up from the back. "Me too? I don't want to stay in the car. Please."

Shelby considered her request before replying, "Don't touch anything."

The trio got out of the cruiser and approached the van. Its tires were blown out, its body covered in what appeared to be bullet holes. Derek instantly feared for Mel's safety.

Shelby apparently read his mind. "Hang back, will you, Mel?" There was no danger of the girl disobeying—she was wide-eyed with apprehension.

"Someone sure went all Peckinpah on this van," Derek mused.

"Peckinpah?"

"*The Wild Bunch? Straw Dogs?* Nothing?"

Shelby shook her head.

"Well, I've got to tell you, Shelby," he said, kicking the dirt. "As family reunions go, this is a bit of a bust."

"Go take a closer look."

Her cryptic replies were starting to irk him. Derek tentatively approached the vehicle. He touched one of the pits in the metal. Nope, no bullet made this hole. It looked as if someone had taken to the van with an ice pick. A hundred ice picks.

"I don't get it," he said, running his hand across the van's side. "I don't know what did this, and I don't know why you brought me here."

"Don't you?" Shelby removed her sunglasses, and her

expression was steely. She had her "don't mess with me" stare on.

Derek was too busy checking out his hand to catch the full implication of Shelby's question. He rubbed his fingers against his palm, and his skin felt...sticky.

"What's that again?" he asked.

Shelby moved in on him so quickly his radar went off. So did Mel's.

"Aunt Shelby?" his daughter asked, her voice trembling.

"This..." Shelby waved at the pockmarked van, "...has *you* written all over it."

Derek stared at her, uncomprehending. When he finally put two and two together, he let loose a laugh that echoed across the plain.

"You think this is funny?" Shelby fumed. She turned to Mel. "Stay put."

She grabbed Derek by the arm and led him around the van. What awaited him on the other side made him blanch.

Dark maroon handprints decorated the van's side like eerie, ancient cave paintings. Blood smeared the door handles, giving a hint to what happened to the vehicle's owner.

"Dear God," Derek whispered.

Shelby went in for the kill. "An abandoned van, puncture marks up and down the length of it, and these..." She waved her hand at the bloody prints. "You want to fess up now and save us both the trouble?"

"Okay, Shel. You win. I'm officially stumped."

"That storm that blew through yesterday may have wiped away some of the evidence, but not all," Shelby said, stepping past him and opening the van's sliding door. As she did so, a flood of flyers fell onto the dusty ground.

Derek picked one up, and the penny dropped.

Stratton's Odditorium: The Strangest Place on Earth.

"I can explain."

"Go ahead." His sister-in-law was all ears.

"Some college students came by looking for some old topo maps I had. Didn't have any cash, so I made a swap: pass out flyers at the festival in exchange for the map. What's the big deal?"

"One student is lying over at Mercy Hospital in a coma," Shelby said. "And another one is missing."

Derek's fists clenched. "You think I did this?"

"I think you know more than you're saying. I think anyone who faked an alien kidnapping—"

"That was a viral marketing strategy for the Odditorium!"

"And left enormous footprints all over the mayor's front lawn—"

"I was just trying to rustle up some business," Derek said, laughing in disbelief.

"These stunts of yours may seem funny to you, but some-times they get people hurt." Shelby's voice began to quiver. "People like my sister."

Derek shook his head. "We're done here."

He rounded the van and collected his daughter.

"What's wrong, Dad?"

"Get in the car."

"But I want to show you something first—"

He opened the rear door. "I said, get in."

Mel did as she was told, removing her backpack and setting it on the seat before getting in herself.

Derek and Shelby were as silent as they'd been driving out. As they approached town, Shelby leaned over to Derek and said, "If that other kid doesn't show up soon, I'm throwing you in jail faster than a wildfire in dry grass."

SEVEN

Marion Kohl sat dumbfounded as she watched her husband eat, thinking, *How in the world did I end up with this man?*

They'd grabbed subs from the little shop off the highway, along with a big bag of honey-dipped pork rinds and stale powdered donuts. Her husband, Oren, sat across from her at the picnic table, wolfing down his sandwich. Marion, in turn, looked out at the beautiful lake set here among the foothills. They had the place to themselves—the mountains were all theirs, and there was no one else around to claim the brilliant blue sky.

But Oren didn't notice any of it. He was too busy shoving food down his piehole.

Marion had looked forward to the vacation all winter. Oren had wanted to go to Vegas, but she'd put her foot down. She hadn't taught for thirty years to watch him make googly eyes at barmaids and fan dancers.

"Let's compromise," she'd said. "We'll go west, but only as far as Colorado."

Oren, who loathed leaving his beloved New Jersey, had pushed back. "What's in Colorado? Nothing but bears and fires."

"If you let me take you to Colorado this year, I'll let you take me to Vegas next year."

There was a lot of hemming and hawing on Oren's part, but eventually, he'd agreed. "But *next* year, we're going for *two* weeks, not one."

"Of course, dear."

Little did Marion's husband know that there would be no Vegas trip next year. She'd already had some rather lengthy conversations with a lawyer. Come September, she was filing for divorce.

"You want some?" Oren asked, holding out the bag of pork rinds. He spat bits of lettuce when he talked.

"I'm good," Marion said.

"You sure? These are honey-dipped. Never saw honey-dipped before."

"I'll pass," she said with a fake smile. Instead, she watched a pair of birds chase each other across the surface of the lake. How happy and carefree they seemed. Perhaps that could be her again someday. After the divorce. After Oren.

"Suit yourself." Her husband ripped open the bag and stuck in a beefy hand. He extracted a giant handful and went to town. The crunching noises punctuated Marion's decision to leave. If she didn't, she'd be condemned to another thirty years with the munching man opposite her.

When had things gone wrong, she wondered and almost laughed aloud at the thought. She might as well ask when had things ever gone right. They were a mismatch from the start, she and Oren. She enjoyed her book club; he enjoyed bowling. She liked to find new spots to eat; he liked bowling. Her idea of a good time was wandering through museums, watching documentaries about famous artists, filling the house with music of all kinds. Oren? Give him a hot dog, a bottle of beer, and a bowling ball, and he was perfectly content.

She could offer him one out of the three on this trip—the ShakesBeer Festival was awash with cold beer. She on the other hand, planned on losing herself in the artistic aspects of the event. She would take in a play or two—*Julius Caesar* was a particular favorite of hers—indulge in unnecessary purchases, and revel in the Shakespearean atmosphere of it all.

Oren grunted as he bit down on a particularly hard bit of pork rind.

"Agh! Damn near cracked my tooth."

"Maybe you should put those away for a bit."

Oren held tight to the bag. "Nothing doing. These are amazing."

Marion sighed and snatched the snacks away, setting them aside. "You won't be saying that if we have to make an emergency trip to the dentist."

Oren looked hurt, like a kid who'd been denied dessert. But that was one thing about Oren: he would *not* be denied. He turned his attention to the cellophane-wrapped donuts and ripped the packaging open with his teeth in defiance.

September couldn't come soon enough.

Marion rose, leaving her husband to his feast, and picked her way down to the rocky shore. She squatted at the water's edge and stuck in her fingers. The lake was ice cold and just about as pure as when the world was born, no doubt. *Giardia be damned,* she thought. She wanted to drink it down in great handfuls, let it freeze her solid because she suddenly knew she couldn't wait until autumn. The words "I want a divorce" were creeping up her throat, and she didn't think she had the power to overcome them.

She stood and flicked the water from her hands.

"Oren?" Marion said in a voice she didn't quite recognize. "We need to talk—"

A bird zipped past her head. Had it swooped a couple of inches to the right, and it would have plowed straight into her. Her sister Misty who lived down in Taos was always saying how everything in life was a sign. A cat scratches at your door? That's a sign. A tree falls on your neighbor's garage? That's a sign. She wondered what Misty would have to say about a bird nearly knocking your block off.

She was about to pick up where she'd left off when she noticed the bird hovering in the air over Oren's head.

"Talk? About what?"

"I..." Marion stood staring in wonder. She'd seen hummingbirds that hovered like that as they sought out nectar. But the more she looked, the more she was certain that it was no bird.

"Hello? Marion?"

Oren waved a greasy hand, trying to get her attention, but the only attention he got was from the thing buzzing overhead.

Buzzing...it can't be...a bee?

But it was. And it was the size of a pigeon. A *big* freaking pigeon.

The creature wasn't just an enlarged copy of your garden variety bee. Its eyes were mirrored like a disco ball. The yellow and black stripes down its abdomen shimmered as well, and for a second Marion considered the notion that what she was looking at was not in fact a living thing but a drone made of metal and plastic.

Marion glanced back at her husband. He was back at the pork rinds, having had his fill of donuts. And the grease on his hand consisted of oil and...

"Honey, put the bag down."

Oren shook his head. "If you tried these, you'd know why that's not happening."

"Oren!"

"What?"

The giant bee dove straight for him. He barely had time to register what was happening before the monstrous thing landed on his outstretched hand, grabbed on with legs as thick as a lobster's, and stabbed him with its stinger. Marion looked on in horror as the barb pierced his palm. Then, the bug tore itself loose, leaving its stinger pulsating in her husband's flesh.

Oren stared in disbelief. "Marion?"

Marion didn't move, didn't *want* to move. The sight of the enormous bee stinging her husband was bad enough, but what was happening to his hand was even worse.

Oren's fingers began to swell, plumping up like hot dogs on a grill. Then his palm expanded, turning an angry crimson. Oren was equal parts perplexed and dismayed. He shook his injured appendage as if he could shake the swelling away. His arm was bloating as well—the venom was working its way inward.

Marion leaped into action. She grabbed up a wad of napkins and pressed it against the exposed section of stinger sprouting from Oren's skin. The bee lay next to her husband on the bench, twitching in the throes of death. Good.

"Hold on," she said in the kindest voice she'd used toward Oren in a long time. "This might hurt."

Might? He's probably going to pass out.

She gripped fleshy stub and yanked. The stinger slipped out easily.

The swelling was another matter. Oren's forearm was as engorged as Popeye's. Now, his lips were puffing up. She knew for a fact they didn't have any Benadryl in their luggage—neither she nor her husband suffered allergies like the rest of the world. Things were going south fast. She had to get him to the hospital *now*.

"Don't worry, honey. I think I remember seeing a clinic down near the Shell station."

Oren responded with a strangled gurgle, his tongue protruding from his mouth.

Marion grabbed her purse and rounded the picnic table to help Oren to his feet when she noticed a black fog rolling across the lake toward them. In the time it took for her to realize that it was no fog bank heading their way but a cloud of bees, the swarm was upon them.

Barbed legs scratched at Marion's skin, and stingers plunged deep. She'd had acupuncture once for a ruptured disc—this was acupuncture on steroids.

She gripped her husband's swollen hand as the swarm embraced her. As the insects stabbed her over and over, she thought of Julius Caesar and the murderous senators. She'd never make it to the play. She'd never make it off this mountain. She'd never...

A particularly pissed bee alighted on Marion's chin, and as she screamed, it crawled into her mouth, buzzing angrily as it burrowed down her throat.

Et tu, Brute? she thought and let go of Oren's hand.

EIGHT

Derek stared out the window during their journey back home, still fuming that Shelby considered him a suspect in the college kid's disappearance. Didn't she know him better than that? Was she getting pressure from her superiors?

There had been a period after Molly's death when Shelby urged him to consider letting her raise Mel. What had pissed him off the most about her arguments was that they made sense. He wasn't the most stable breadwinner. A roadside attraction wasn't exactly the ideal place to raise a child. And the kicker was that Shelby loved the daylights out of Mel. He was certain Shelby saw a lot of Molly in the girl, just like he did.

"Why isn't anybody talking?" Mel said, fidgeting in the back seat. She had her backpack perched atop her lap and held it there like it was a comfort animal.

It was Shelby who answered. "I don't know about your dad, but I've got a lot on my mind."

"Like what? Police stuff?"

"Yeah," Shelby said, throwing a look Derek's way. "Police stuff."

"You mean like that?" Derek asked as they headed up the dusty drive to the Odditorium. An official vehicle, a massive Police Responder, was parked out front and a man stood at its side, sunlight reflecting off his glasses.

"I don't know what *that* is," Shelby said, slowing as they approached. She sounded sincere enough, but Derek was too far down the paranoia rabbit hole.

"Sure you don't."

"What's that supposed to mean?"

Derek didn't reply, just kept his eyes on the man standing outside his home.

Shelby pulled over parallel to the other vehicle and put the cruiser into park. "Stay here. Let me do the talking."

"I thought you'd say that." Derek opened his door and stepped outside. "What can I do for you, Chief? Why do I get the impression you aren't here to buy a ticket?"

Chief Cross, a rugged man with the face of an old western cowboy and hat to match, held up a folded document, the paper fluttering in the wind.

"Derek Stratton, you're being evicted."

"On whose authority? I thought evictions were the sheriff's domain."

"I'm saving him the trouble. Next time you decide to let your payments slide, make damn sure your landlord ain't the mayor."

Derek sauntered up to the man and accepted the paper. "Come on, Chief. Why don't you go back and tell the mayor I'll write her a check tomorrow?"

Cross spat tobacco juice, and the wind carried it dangerously close to Derek's face. "Tell her yourself."

"Chief…" Shelby chimed in.

"You don't want to get messed up in this, Officer," the man said. He turned to Mel, who was pressed up against the rear passenger window. He tipped his hat at her, revealing a cue ball dome, before returning to his vehicle and firing it up. As the police vehicle sped off down the drive, it kicked up a cloud of dust that scattered in the rising wind.

"Just great," Derek said, holding up his eviction notice. "Thanks for this."

"I didn't know what we were walking into."

"Really?" Derek smiled *way* too broadly. "Kind of a pretty big co-inky-dinky, if you ask me."

Shelby stood firm. "I'm telling you an eviction wasn't on my radar."

Derek made note of the fact that his sister-in-law put a hand on her hip when she was emphatic. Just like Molly. And despite the sunglasses, he could tell she was speaking the truth.

It didn't matter. He tried to open the rear door and found it locked. "Would you mind releasing my daughter?"

"God, Derek, do you always have to be so dramatic?" Still, she went to the driver's side and unlocked the rear doors. Mel crawled out, shouldered her pack, and headed toward the building. "Mel?"

"She doesn't like yelling," Derek said, folding up the notice. "That's something you'd know if you ever came by."

"If I was ever invited, don't you mean?"

"Oh, please."

Shelby fished around in her pocket and came up with a small roll of bills. She handed it to Derek.

"I don't want your money."

"It's not for you. It's for Mel—"

"I know what it's for."

Shelby reached over and stuffed the money in Derek's shirt pocket. "I missed her last birthday. The least I can do is help her go on her bug hunt, or whatever the hell it is."

The two had quickly found themselves at loggerheads, and Derek didn't have the energy for this conversation.

"Fine. But you tell your boss I'm not budging. Not one damn inch."

"Look, if you want me and Justine to take Mel while you sort this out—"

Derek ripped up the notice and tossed the shredded pieces at her. It didn't have the effect he wanted. The wind was really picking up, and the bits of paper swirled upward and disappeared. With his parting shot gone bust, he decided to end the conversation with a spiteful "Ha!" and headed off, leaving Shelby standing there in the drive, gray clouds rolling in behind her.

When Derek entered their little apartment, Mel was sitting at the kitchen table with a multicolored popsicle.

"Dad, are we being evicted?"

"Not if I have anything to do about it."

"You're sure?"

"I'm sure, honey. Why don't you watch a little TV?" He

wanted her attention elsewhere. He had business to attend to.

"TV's boring. I have something I want to show you."

Derek just wanted to get to the Odditorium. He'd tasted something in the air that excited a primal part of his brain— the part that made ninety-nine percent of the human race run for cover. He was in the lucky/unlucky one percent.

"Can it wait?"

"Yeah."

"I'll look a little later, okay?"

"Okay."

Derek kissed his daughter on the head and felt the warmth of her hair on his lips. His mind wanted to drag him down to the maudlin depths, but he wasn't having any of that. Not right now. The sky was churning something up. He needed to be ready.

"Make us both a sandwich. Can you do that?" Anything to keep her busy.

"Ham and cheese?"

"Perfect." He paused, removed Shelby's money from his pocket, and set it on the kitchen table. "Your aunt says happy birthday."

"My birthday's in March."

"I know."

With that, Derek crossed the room and unlatched the door to the Odditorium.

The NOAA radio Molly had given him on their fifth anniversary was covered in dust, but it came to life when he switched it on. Derek sat at his workbench in the utility room, where he kept things like spare eyeballs for the mannequins and gels for the lights, and listened intently to the automated voice squawking from the radio.

"The National Weather Service in Denver has issued a tornado warning for southwestern Butte County in northeast Colorado until 3:30 p.m., mountain daylight time."

Thunder rolled overhead, loud enough to cause the old chandelier Derek had salvaged from an old theater to tinkle a warning.

"At 1:41 p.m., National Weather Service Doppler radar indicated a line of severe thunderstorms..."

That clinched it. Derek rushed out of the utility room and into the exhibition hall. He zipped past the Tommyknocker display and knocked over the Slide Rock Bolter sign—*Part-Whale, Part-Monster, All Horror!*—on his way to his destination. And when he found himself in front of the Tornado Suit, he knew what he had to do.

———

Mel was shaking potato chips onto paper plates to accompany the turkey sandwiches she'd made—a last-minute substitution since the ham had turned green and slimy—when she heard the VW's motor roar to life.

She ran to the door and flung it open. The sky was aswirl like a watercolor come to life. Great flashes illuminated the clouds, and hail began to fall. The *Lightning Bug* sped down the drive, the Tornado Suit strapped to its back. Into the storm.

"No," Mel whispered.

NINE

The plan was simple: get ahead of the storm, suit up, and pray for a twister to drop.

"Simple. Ha!" Derek snorted as the Beetle's wiper blades did battle with the hail. He hoped he wouldn't have to brake anytime soon. The "new" tires he'd put on the VW were about as bald as Chief Cross. If he hit the brake pedal, he'd probably end up sliding into the next county.

The Tornado Suit proved to be in good working order. Its cameras fired up when he plugged in the suit's battery pack—the pack had been charging since before Molly's demise, he realized. The oxygen tanks were unused and ready to go. The only element he had any questions about was the user.

This is going to work, this is going to work...

It had to. The future of his broken little family depended upon it. If he could sell Mix footage of the suit in action, he could stop the financial bleeding and maybe, just maybe, start the slow climb back to normalcy.

Normalcy? What did that even mean? Heck, Mel was

doing a better job of adjusting than he was. Or at least, she was better at pretending.

"If this works," he said to the storm, "I promise to be a better father. I promise to be a better man. I promise, I promise..."

The storm must have heard him as it loosed a tremendous streak of lightning in reply. The hail was abating, but he wasn't worried. He knew tornado weather like some folks knew fishing spots, and his inner compass pointed him onward.

The Beetle coughed, and Derek momentarily panicked. The last thing he needed was for the *Lightning Bug* to conk out on him. He gave the car more gas, and the VW cleared its throat, leaving a cloud of black exhaust behind. But the little Beetle zoomed on, as intent as he was to get ahead of the storm.

He flipped on the shortwave radio mounted to the dash.

"Locations in the warning include, but are not limited to, Harkness, Long Feather and Fort Womack. The safest place to be during a tornado is a basement. If no basement is available to you..."

"Then you're SOL," Derek said.

He was out on the grasslands now, the foothills to his right bracing for the approaching tempest. The landscape looked familiar, and it wasn't until he reached the outcropping of rock jutting from the field that he realized where he was. Although the college students' van was nowhere to be seen, crime scene tape still fluttered in the wind, trapped by rocks.

Is this kismet? he wondered.

Molly loved contemplating synchronicity. Before they fell

asleep, she'd carry on lengthy monologues about how the entire universe was just one big machine, and everything that happened was part of its design. Derek would usually cut her spiels short by switching on the sound machine he kept on his bedside table.

"Am I boring you?" she'd ask.

"Never," he'd reply. "Let's go to sleep."

Now he wished he'd tossed that damn machine in the trash and let her talk to her heart's content.

He quickly parked the Beetle and got out. The sky was gearing up to deliver something big. Whether that was a twister or a torrential downpour remained to be seen. In either case, it was time to get busy.

First, he set up the old camcorder on a tripod, hit record, and trained it on the sky.

"Okay, folks. Here we have the birth of a twister. What an awesome sight," he said, playing narrator. "We have darkening skies, the hail just passed, and the wind is kicking up dust. Wish I could stay and chat, but I've got to get dressed for work." He turned the camera on himself and stared into the lens. "This one's for you, honey."

He turned the camcorder off and tossed it and the tripod into the back seat of the Beetle before rushing around to the back of the vehicle where the Tornado Suit awaited.

Derek detached the bungees holding the suit in place. It had taken every ounce of strength to secure it to the back of the car in the first place—it was a two-man job. As he released the last bungee, the suit crumpled to the ground like a drunken tin man.

As he rolled the suit over, unclasping clasps and unbuckling buckles, a sound like a giant approaching caught his attention. The storm was whipping itself up into a lather.

He had his tin man, he had his storm—all he needed was a twister and he was off to see the wizard.

I do *believe in kismet, I* do *believe in kismet...*

A dark wisp of cloud dropped as the sky rewarded him with a funnel. The twister descended like a great fang, eager to take a bite out of the world.

Right on cue.

Derek flicked on the suit's myriad cameras and made sure they were recording. He tested out the helmet's mic, the oxygen, and the beacon. All systems go.

The twister was turning into a monster, and he suddenly realized what those characters in *Jaws* must have felt like, staring into the mouth of death.

He wriggled into the suit, tumbleweeds pelting him and the Beetle. Derek's grief had caused him to put on a few extra pounds—mint chip ice cream will do that. As a result, he ended up having to squeeze himself into the suit.

"Come on, man. Suck it in."

He pulled the helmet over his head and locked it tight. A loud suction sound echoed in his ears.

"All right, folks. Yours truly is locked into the Tornado Suit. Let's see what kind of trouble we can get into, okay?"

With that, he headed across the grassy plain toward the massive funnel. His breath came in short gasps, and he tried to calm himself. It was no use. This was what he'd been working for—*they'd* been working for—for the better part of a decade. So, as the twister locked him in its sights, he did likewise.

"Wind is picking up," he said into the mic. "I'm going to

keep talking for as long as I can. This thing is breathtaking. It's heaven and hell wrapped into one. It's..."

He trailed off as he realized something else that the tornado was—it was veering off to the west.

"No, no, no!" he shouted, launching into action. The suit was never meant to offer its wearer any more than a rudimentary ability to move. Now, he was asking it to let him run, and the suit was having none of it. "Come on!"

The twister bore down, ripping up chunks of land as it came. If Derek had been driving the Beetle, he could have sped into its path, but he was on foot, clanking away in a suit never meant for speed. Every step was an effort—he felt like he was in a nightmare where no matter how hard he tried, he couldn't put one foot in front of the other fast enough.

The suit's right knee joint locked up. As Derek took the next step, the frozen leg caused him to lose balance, and he toppled over, landing on his side.

Cursing, he rocked back and forth until finally ending up on his belly. Grabbing at clumps of scrub grass, Derek pulled himself toward the funnel. Sweat poured down his face with the strain, but all he could do was watch as the towering twister roared past. He screamed, hurling every obscenity in the book in his sorrow and rage, tears rolling down his cheeks.

A piece of debris caught on his helmet, obscuring his view.

Not only did I miss my shot, now I can't even see the blasted thing.

He reached up with his metal mesh glove and tried to brush the debris away, but it held firm. He tried to grab it, but it crawled out of his grasp.

Crawled?

He squinted, focusing on the obstruction; the obstruction stared right back. Grabbing the thing with both hands, he ripped it from his helmet and threw it tumbling to the ground.

The bee righted itself and glared at him defiantly.

Derek froze.

When he was a child growing up in Indiana, his mother had been an avid gardener. She was also allergic to everything under the sun. No matter how hot it was, Millicent Stratton would cover herself in clothing from head to toe, including a sun hat, gloves, and two pairs of socks, whenever she and her young son ventured into the backyard. She passed her phobia of poison ivy, poison oak, and biting ticks to her son, but nothing was so infectious as his mother's fear of bees.

Early one spring, when Derek was no more than four, his mother accidentally disturbed a hive of honeybees while trying to unearth a small stump. The swarm had risen, angry and reproachful, and Millicent Stratton had turned to her son and yelled, "Bees! Run!"

The memory burned itself into the very structure of young Derek's gray matter. From that moment on, the word "bee" had the same connotation as "fire" or "active shooter." And so, as Derek recognized the thing crawling across his visor, his heart nearly exploded.

Bee! Run!

Gravity proved no match for a man scared out of his wits. Derek was back up and running, clanking away like Dorothy's tin companion escaping the flying monkeys. Fear racing through his veins, he temporarily forgot about the twister and why he'd trapped himself inside the suit in the first place.

He also forgot to look where he was going.

His steel boot struck a clump of sandstone jutting from the ground, and he went down for a second time, jarring his bones in the process. When Derek saw where he'd landed, he caught his breath. He teetered over the edge of a great crevasse—an enormous scar running hundreds of feet on either side of him. Had he fallen a few more inches forward, he'd be tumbling down into the bowels of the earth.

He crawled as best he could back from the edge, a difficult thing to do with the wind whipping about him. The vortex was passing on his right, tearing up the world, and he was in the debris cloud. Rocks and brush pummeled him, battering the suit, threatening to crush it with him inside.

"I'm sorry," he cried. Whether he was speaking to Mel or Molly or the Lord above, he didn't rightly know.

As he lay there, pressed to the ground, he spied something emerging from the crevasse, antennae first. It was followed by another and another, and his greatest nightmare was realized. Hundreds...no, thousands of enormous bees were crawling out of the earth.

Derek screamed until he could no longer hear himself screaming. One by one, the colossal insects took to the air, only to be caught in the updraft of the passing giant. The tornado was heading south, and the swarm followed, either in pursuit of the rest of their colony or in a misguided attempt to attack the departing twister. So great were they in number that they further darkened the raging tornado.

Then, as quickly as the funnel had formed, it began to dissipate. The vortex lost its shape and began to spin out, tossing wisps of cloud and pockets of bees to the wind. In a matter of seconds, the mighty force of nature was gone, and the swarm, no doubt disoriented by their journey up into the tornado, dropped from the sky like rain, plummeting toward the earth.

Before they struck the ground, the bees regained control and veered upward. Unlike an undulating murmuration of birds, their formation was uniform, precise. The swarm moved in a great arc, spinning slowly on a central axis. The bees were forming their own twister.

Lightning crackled along the surface of the newly formed funnel, making it look like a massive electric sculpture.

This time, Derek was directly in the twister's path. The bees roared over the Beetle. The little car quaked beneath the barrage of bees. The VW rose into the vortex, drawn upward into the buzzing cloud.

Derek watched in horror as the vehicle spun about in the swarm, disappearing and reappearing. Suddenly, the VW broke free and plummeted downward.

He curled into a ball as the vehicle smashed to the ground next to him, windows shattering, its horn stuck and blaring as if in pain.

Before the swarm reached Derek, the funnel began to wobble, losing its cohesion. A moment later, the swarm abandoned its formation, and bees scattered across the sky. Derek tried to still his racing heart as the cloud of insects raced off, leaving him spent on the dusty ground.

"That," he whispered to himself as the bees disappeared from view, "was a damn bee tornado."

TEN

After ripping out the wiring to the Beetle's horn and working some magic under the hood, Derek managed to get the vehicle running. The *Lightning Bug* had seen better days—its surface was peppered with sting marks, the only window that remained was the rear, and every time he tried to get it to go over fifty, it sounded like the *1812 Overture*. The Tornado Suit was in no better shape than the Beetle—it hung lifeless, strapped to the back of the car, clanging with each bump.

Derek had taken a quick look at the footage from the cameras mounted to the suit, and viewing it had caused him to relive the horror. Sure, a lot of it was shaky, but there were moments when the tornado was clearly visible. More than that, he had caught the bee tornado's birth.

He had to show Shelby. Had to warn her. He dialed as he drove, but per usual, she let the call go to voicemail. Switching gears, he called Mel.

"Hey, Dad. Where are—"

"I need to make this quick, Melissa," he shouted over the

wind, using her full name to ensure she paid careful attention. "I'm okay. I'm heading into town. Do you have something for lunch?"

"I made us sandwiches, but you didn't eat yours."

"Well, you can have mine for dinner if I'm home late. I just need to take care of something."

"But Dad!"

"Yeah? What is it?"

There was silence on the other end of the line. Then Mel sighed. "Nothing, Dad."

"Love you."

"Love—"

Derek hit the gas, and the VW's engine bellowed like it was angry with the world.

By the time Derek pulled up in front of the Fort Womack Police Station, his car was ready to call it quits. He quickly parked, grabbed up the cameras' memory cards and the camcorder's tape, and stuffed them in his pockets.

Two festival-goers who looked like they had just stepped out of the worst community theater production of *Romeo and Juliet* stopped to marvel at his hissing Beetle.

"Dude, your car's toast," Romeo said.

"You're telling me," Derek replied as he ascended the steps to the station.

The Fort Womack station was hopping. The festival was in full swing, and the police had their hands full. A drunken, bearded man in Elizabethan garb, complete with tights, fended off a couple of cops with an obviously plastic sword.

"Unhand me, you scoundrels! You knaves!" the bearded man slurred with a swish of his sword. "I must needs return to the stage. My audience awaits!"

"Looks like this is your understudy's lucky day," an officer said, extracting his cuffs.

"Thou blackguard! Thou rogue! You mean to manacle me, sirrah?" The man lunged. "Have at you!"

Chief Cross stepped calmly from his office and walked up to the howling thespian. "Put the toy down."

The man whirled on the chief, sword upraised. "I think not, Constable!"

Cross grabbed the man's sword and broke it across his knee. He snatched the cuffs from the officer's hands and quickly subdued the actor, cuffing his hands behind his back.

"Get this ham out of here," Cross growled.

Mayor Guffey wheeled herself out of the chief's office. The mayor was a striking middle-aged woman with a severe haircut. She wielded her wheelchair with authority and a total disregard for others' feet. The police department might have been Cross's domain, but Mayor Guffey was the boss of any room she entered.

"Chief Cross? Do you mind? We haven't finished our meeting."

"Sorry, ma'am," Cross said. "Just taking out the trash."

"I want you to get the temporary cages set up," the mayor snapped. "That should be able to handle the overflow. If we have just one incident like those topless riders at the bike rally, those bastards in Denver are going to put our summer grants on the chopping block."

"You got it."

Having had her say, the mayor headed for the exit. Derek saw his opportunity, and he took it.

"Mayor! Chief Cross! A word."

Cross took one look at Derek and shook his head. "This day just keeps getting better and better."

"I have nothing to say to you, Mr. Stratton," Mayor Guffey said. "Vacate my property. Now."

In his haste to deliver his warning, Derek had forgotten all about his impending eviction. "That's not why I'm here."

The mayor snapped her fingers at the chief. "Would you mind?"

"Not at all." Cross headed Derek off at the pass, herding him toward the door.

"You need to listen to me," Derek insisted.

"And you need to leave."

Derek planted himself in the doorway. "There's a swarm of giant killer bees just south of town. And I've got proof! Bees!"

He pulled the memory cards from his pocket and held them aloft. The whole room simply stared at him.

"Chief, give me your Taser," Mayor Guffey ordered.

"Ma'am..."

"Someone give me a damn Taser!"

Derek held out the memory cards to Cross. "Take a look. One look is all I ask."

"You've got a lot of nerve pulling a stunt on a busy day like today," the mayor said.

"This is no stunt," Derek cried. "You've got to trust me. If you don't listen to me, people are going to die. And it's going to be on *your* head."

The chief crossed the room in mere seconds. He snatched

the memory cards from Derek's outstretched hand and dropped them in the wastebasket. Cross twirled Derek about and slammed him face-first against the wall.

"You always gotta do things the hard way, eh Stratton?"

"Lock him up until Monday!" Mayor Guffey snarled. "Until the festival is over, and he's had time to remember his manners."

The chief was going for his own cuffs when Shelby entered the room. She took one look at Derek and Cross and sighed.

"What's going on here?"

"Your brother-in-law's just begging me to toss him in a holding cell," Cross said, giving Derek a shove for good measure.

Shelby let out a breath. "Mind if I take it from here?"

"Suit yourself." Cross turned Derek to face him. "You just caught a break, but you listen and listen good. If any of my boys see you within spitting distance of the festival, I'll make sure you spend the rest of summer eating prison food. Got it?"

"Got it." Derek retrieved the memory cards from the trash and stormed out the door.

Derek took the steps two at a time and yanked open the Beetle's door. Shelby was right behind him.

"What's wrong with you? Seriously, Derek?"

Derek got in the car and stuck his head out the window. "I know you don't like me. I know you think I got your sister killed."

"Derek..."

"I also know what put that kid in the hospital."

"And what would that be?"

Derek swallowed hard before answering. "Bees." He spread his hands wide. "Big, *big* bees."

Shelby rolled her eyes.

"Oh, come on, Derek—"

"It's true!"

"You've cried wolf too many times."

Derek steeled himself. "If I'm lying, I'll give you and Justine custody of Melissa."

Shelby folded her arms. "Show me your proof."

Derek turned the ignition—the car cleared its throat. "Get in."

Shelby gave the battered VW a once-over. "I'll follow you. Just in case you lose any parts along the way."

The lack of a windshield made listening to the radio a nonstarter. Derek instead concentrated on the whistling wind as he sped back home to the Odditorium. Shelby followed behind in her cruiser, providing him with his own personal escort.

Where had the swarm come from? How had they grown to such monstrous proportions? Why the hell had they formed a tornado? All good questions; so few answers. He needed Molly. She was his sounding board—together, they could figure out anything. He was out of his depth. He needed an ally. He needed to convince Shelby of his sincerity, but she was right. His stock and trade was crying wolf, pulling the wool over people's eyes. He'd always fancied himself the PT Barnum of the Rockies. Now, his reputation was coming back to bite him.

Derek pulled down the drive to the Odditorium, picking gnats out of his teeth. Proof. If that was what Shelby needed, he'd give it to her. All he had to do was show her the footage, and he'd have a new ally—an ally with a badge.

He rolled to a halt at the back of the building, the Beetle's brakes having gone squishy during its tangle with the bees. He leaped out and headed for the door.

"Come on," Derek called back to Shelby. "You have *got* to see this."

With that, he threw open the door to the apartment.

Hovering in front of him at eye level was a bee the size of a lobster. One of Molly's knitting needles pierced its thorax, and yet it hung there in midair, buzzing its warning, its legs clicking in anticipation of its attack.

Mel appeared in the doorway behind the airborne insect.

"Don't let it get away, Dad!"

"Holy...Mel! Close the door."

"But, Dad—"

"Do it!"

His daughter obeyed, slamming the door closed. Derek stumbled backward. The bee pursued him. Could bees smell fear? It really didn't matter. Whatever pheromones Derek was putting out, the bee was keen to follow.

With the bee buzzing ever closer, Derek did what anyone would do in that situation: he hauled off and punched it as hard as he could. He connected but only managed to startle the thing. And piss it off.

"Now do you believe me?" he called to Shelby. How was it staying aloft, skewered as it was?

"Drop!"

"What?"

He looked over at Shelby. She was motioning for him to get on the ground.

"Drop!"

Derek dropped, sitting unceremoniously on the ground before lying flat. The bee hovered over him, both knitting needle and stinger poised at his head.

Shelby's firearm went off, startling Derek. Her aim was true—the bee took a hit in the side. Amazingly, one shot wasn't enough. The second dealt the creature a mortal hit, nearly splitting it in two.

The bee plummeted, landing directly on Derek's chest. It squirmed, tarsal claws biting through his shirt, and then it was still.

Shelby walked up to him, blotting out the sun. Derek stared up at her, bee goo dripping down his chest.

"I told you so," Derek said.

"You're welcome," Shelby replied, holstering her pistol.

ELEVEN

"Where did you find this?" Derek held the dead bee by the steel needle on which it was impaled.

Mel sat before him on the sofa, feet crossed, eyes down.

"Next to the van," his daughter whispered.

"The van I took your father to see?" Shelby asked.

Mel nodded.

"Why didn't you tell me about it?" Derek asked.

"I tried to! You didn't listen."

"Why is it stuck on one of Mom's knitting needles?" Derek held out the bee—Mel wouldn't look at it.

"It was for my bug collection."

"What bug collection?"

Mel looked him in the eye. She'd been close to tears, but no more. His daughter was steamed.

"Don't you listen to anything I say?"

"Look here, young lady—"

"I was going to have the *best* bug out of everybody..." Mel turned to Shelby, her wrath not yet spent, "and *you* had to shoot it. Now it's ruined."

Derek looked at the bee kebab he was holding. That last shot had taken out half its legs and a good deal of its guts. Other than its hallmark large size, it was in pretty rough shape.

"Mel..." Derek said.

"I thought it was dead, okay? I thought it was dead, and I stuck it in my backpack. I'm sorry. Can I go to my room now?"

"Not yet," Shelby said.

"Yes," Derek insisted, overriding her.

Mel got up from the sofa and sulked all the way to her bedroom. Derek expected her to slam the door behind her, and he wasn't disappointed.

He quickly set the bee down on the kitchen table. "I have to wash my hands."

"Change your shirt while you're at it," Shelby recommended.

Derek looked down at his shirtfront. It was smeared orange and brown with bee guts.

"Damn."

He quickly swapped the shirt out for an old Odditorium T-shirt—*Grand Opening of the Oddest Place on Earth!*—and tossed the soiled garment into the trash before washing up in the kitchen sink.

"This *can't* be real," Shelby said. She was examining the bee carcass with a pen as one would study a magic trick, trying to discern its secrets.

Derek checked out the fridge and offered her a bottle of Coke. Shelby passed.

"When it comes to making people believe the unbelievable, I'm good. Really good. This?" He toasted the dead bee with his beverage. "I couldn't fake this in a million years."

"Show me the footage you took."

"Gladly."

Derek sat at his desk. Mel usually worked the computer for him, but he managed to upload the video files from the memory cards. When he was done, he waved Shelby over.

"This first clip is from the camera mounted on my left shoulder."

He hit play.

Shaky footage of the tornado appeared on the monitor. The video was blurry, but Derek's voice came through loud and clear.

"I'm going to keep talking for as long as I can. This thing is breathtaking."

"And this is from the camera on my right."

A second window opened—the video was much clearer, although there was no sound. The tornado was close and ripping up chunks of earth.

"And finally...my helmet cam."

This footage was the sharpest. Derek and Shelby watched as the tornado dissipated and the column of bees rose. When the creatures locked themselves into a funnel formation, Derek heard his sister-in-law gasp.

"You didn't fake this."

"Nope," Derek assured her.

"We need to show this to the chief."

Derek laughed. "Are you serious? He was about to toss me in a cell and throw away the key."

Shelby threw up her hands. "Well, what do you propose?"

Derek was busy attaching the camcorder's cord to the computer. Sure, it was just his introduction—no tornado captured in this footage—but with his luck, if he didn't upload it ASAP, he'd accidentally tape over it. Like he had with Molly.

Connection complete, he began inputting the camcorder's footage.

"When the kid bought that old map off me," Derek said, rising and going to the cupboard, "he mentioned that some crazy old man had sent them my way. I'm pretty sure I know who he was talking about."

He grabbed a jar from one of the shelves and tossed it to Shelby.

"Tom Buckaroo's Organic Raw Honey," she said, reading the label. "Buckaroo...he's that bee guy, isn't he? Justine's always buying his stuff. Lip balm, face scrub."

"And with the ShakesBeer Festival going on, I bet you anything he's slinging mead at his booth right now. If anyone knows what we're dealing with, it's him."

Derek headed for Mel's room. When she didn't answer his knock, he let himself in. His daughter was curled up on her bed, facing the wall.

"Aunt Shelby and I are going to go into town for a bit. Can I trust you to keep your nose clean?"

Mel rolled over. "What does that mean?"

"Will you stay inside and stay out of trouble?"

The girl rolled her eyes in response.

"I'll take that as, 'Of course, Dad.'"

"Of course, Dad," Mel sassed.

Derek gave her a warning finger and kiss on the cheek.

"Back soon."

Shelby stood waiting for him. "If Cross catches you downtown, your ass is grass."

Derek flashed her a smile. "Don't worry. I've got an idea."

TWELVE

Despite the SUV's AC blowing at max, Rose was sweating like a marathon runner. Daisy, who sat dripping beside her, cracked her window an inch.

"Don't you dare," Rose said, overriding her friend's desire for a cool breeze. The passenger-side window slid shut.

"Oh, come on, Rose. It's a sauna in here."

"We've got a couple thousand dollars' worth of flowers in the back," Rose said, putting her foot down. "I, for one, am *not* showing up with pots filled with nothing but stems. The City of Fort Womack is one of our best customers."

Daisy placed her hand on one of the vents. "My God, I think it's actually putting out heat."

"It's not putting out heat."

Daisy redirected the vent in question toward her friend. Rose batted away the hot air. "Okay! Okay!" she said, switching off the air.

"Did you text the mayor yet?" Daisy asked.

"You don't text the mayor, you text her office."

"Well, did you text her office?"

Rose was silent.

"You didn't, did you?" Daisy snapped.

"Let's just get there, okay?"

Daisy fanned herself. "Why didn't you get the AC fixed?"

"Why didn't *you* rent the van?"

This shut Daisy up. Ever since she and her old college roommate had gone into business together, it had been *her* job to manage transportation. While she was usually on top of things, this time she dropped the ball. And she was paying for it in the form of dehydration.

Her oversight was why the two of them were sweltering in Rose's old Pilot decorated with magnetic signs touting their company—Petalicious—instead of riding in the cool comfort of a rental.

"Keep straight on Highway 25 for ten miles," Rose's phone instructed.

Rose was in a particularly dour frame of mind as she drove. Not only had their flower delivery been late, but they were about to pass that delay onto their client. Mayor Guffey had supported their business from the get-go, selecting their small startup over larger, more established florists. The mayor was related to Rose's Uncle Penn by marriage, but Rose liked to think that what may have started as a bit of casual nepotism had blossomed because of the quality service she and Daisy delivered.

But a late delivery, especially for a big event like the ShakesBeer Festival? Rocky Mountain Florists and The Queen of Green would be eager to swoop in and pick up the slack.

Therefore, the windows would remain closed for the

duration of their drive from Loveland to Fort Womack. Rose didn't intend to lose a single petal.

Hot and growing grumpier with every mile, Daisy clicked on the radio. As luck would have it, the classic rock station was playing Glenn Frey's "The Heat is On." Daisy snarled and switched it off.

A *ding* sounded from the dashboard, and a little yellow gas pump signal lit up.

"You've got to be kidding me," Daisy groaned.

"I just filled up on Wednesday," Rose said.

"Unbelievable."

"But I *just* filled up!"

"Well, it's empty!"

A billboard for Westco Convenience appeared up ahead like a sign from God. Rose gave a sigh of relief. A quick stop and they'd be back on their way.

She took the exit, careful on the curve to ensure the flowers' safety and pulled up to the lone pump at Westco. A paper bag covered the pump handle. On it were scrawled the words *NO GAS*.

"Seriously?" Rose snarled.

Daisy opened her door and hopped out. She flapped her arms, trying to dry out her drenched T-shirt.

"We don't have time for that," Rose called.

"Gimme a minute."

"We don't have a minute."

Daisy stood her ground defiantly. "You're more worried about those damn flowers than you are about me."

Rose grumbled. "Get in the car, Daisy."

"And die of heatstroke?"

"No one's going to die," Rose assured her. She opened

and closed her door in rapid succession, airing out the SUV. Her bellows-like motion filled the cab with the overwhelming scent of flowers. "See?"

Daisy reluctantly trudged back to the Pilot and jumped in. She turned to Rose. "Call a mechanic as soon as we make our delivery."

"You got it."

Daisy glanced at the dash. "We have enough gas to get there?"

"I don't know," Rose replied, throwing the SUV in gear. "I've never run her dry."

Daisy wrinkled her nose. "Smells like a funeral home in here."

"The mayor loves lilies."

"Good for her. Let's go."

The Pilot pulled out of the gas station and headed back toward the highway.

"Keep straight on Highway 25 for eight miles," Rose's phone instructed.

"Yeah, yeah, yeah," Rose replied.

High above, a dark cloud rolling from the west suddenly switched directions. It followed the SUV and the sickly-sweet scent of lilies.

THIRTEEN

Tremont Street into Fort Womack was jam-packed with cars trying to get downtown. The line of vehicles came to a standstill as it approached Aspen Avenue, where police had blocked the way to all but foot traffic. Luckily for Derek, Shelby was driving.

His sister-in-law flipped a switch, and the lights atop the cruiser flashed and the siren sounded. Tourists couldn't get out of the way fast enough.

"I should get a siren for the *Lightning Bug*," Derek said.

"No, you most definitely should not."

When they got to the barricades, one of Shelby's fellow officers waved them through, but not before giving Derek a shout-out.

"Looking good, Mr. Squatch!"

Derek gave the man a double thumbs-up. The Bigfoot costume he was wearing was not only hot but itchy as hell. And he could already feel the sweat trickling down his back. Molly had constructed the suit not for wearing but for the Sasquatch display. If Derek had known that one day, he'd have to don the thing so as to avoid being spotted by the chief, he'd have had his wife put in some major ventilation. As it was, he was trapped beneath a patchwork of furs on one of the sunniest days of the year.

"How much farther to the vendors' booths?" he asked.

"Just three blocks down Tremont, but we have to pull over here. Hope you're ready to meet your public."

Shelby pulled over in front of one of Fort Womack's many frozen yogurt joints.

Derek hopped out, accidentally frightening a young girl in a stroller, who began bawling.

"Oh! No cry, no cry! Bigfoot nice!" he said in what he hoped was a non-threatening, monster voice.

Discovering that the hairy creature in front of her could speak only added to the child's terror. She screamed bloody murder, alerting her protective parents.

"Do you mind?" the girl's mother said, grabbing hold of the stroller.

"Sorry," Derek mumbled from beneath the mask.

"Listen up, Mr. Bear—" the child's father said.

"I'm not a bear. I'm Bigfoot."

"Whatever. Go bother someone else's kid."

The perturbed parents shuttled their still-wailing child off into the throng of festivalgoers.

Shelby approached, eyebrows raised. "You're doing a bang-up job blending in."

Derek snatched a cotton grocery bag from the cruiser. The bag contained a gallon-sized mason jar usually reserved for lemonade—crammed inside was the dead bee. "Which way to the booths?"

Shelby pointed down Tremont, where crowds of people

milled about, some in Shakespearean costume pieces, some with plastic cups of beer, some with both. Street corner performers spouted monologues for spare change, while others sang bawdy songs accompanied by lute. Getting through them all would be like parting the Red Sea. Luckily, Derek had his Moses.

"Coming through," Shelby called as they made their way through the masses. "Move aside."

Based on their reactions, Derek was able to identify the underage drinkers among the younger fairgoers. Some tried to conceal their beverages, while others attempted to blend into the crowd, and a few chose to surreptitiously pass their IPAs to older companions.

A young man waved Derek over to his small cluster of friends, all wielding yards of ale. "Bigfoot! Let's get a selfie!"

Taking a selfie with a bunch of drunken college students was the last thing on Derek's list of priorities, but when the crew started chanting *Bigfoot! Bigfoot!* he figured that if a quick photo would shut them up, he'd indulge them.

He tapped Shelby on the shoulder. "Hold up."

The group cheered as he approached, handing him a half-empty yard of golden lager. Derek held it up like a scepter as the friends snapped photo after photo.

"Lemme wear the mask!" one of the more inebriated of the group shouted, making a grab for his head. The man almost succeeded in unmasking him, but Derek quickly ducked away and returned to Shelby's side.

"Always showboating, aren't you?" Shelby said.

"Let's go find Buckaroo. Which one is his booth?"

"There's a directory on the festival website with a map," Shelby said, pulling out her phone and scrolling through the site. "Ugh, why do they all want you to subscribe to their newsletter?"

"Shelby..."

With her attention on her phone, Shelby hadn't heard Derek's whispered warning. She plowed right into the side of a wheelchair.

"I'm so sorry," she began, then froze as she recognized the woman with the wheels.

Derek gave a sudden inhale, accidentally swallowing a mouthful of hair. He tried hacking it up, but it was no use—the hair stuck to the sides of his throat.

Mayor Guffey spun about.

"Officer Parker," the mayor said, a politician's smile on her face. "Enjoying yourself?"

"Yes, I..."

Derek didn't immediately understand Shelby's hesitance. He wanted to tell her to smile and move on. But one look at the members of the press flanking the mayor, and it all made sense.

"This is Officer Parker," Mayor Guffey said to the reporters. "She's one of Fort Womack's finest. It's public servants like her who help keep our town the wonderful, family-friendly place it is."

A cameraman with a sunburned nose turned his attention to Derek. "Hey, Bigfoot! What brings you to the Shakes-Beer Festival?"

All eyes turned Derek's way. Although he was still coughing on the hair he'd swallowed, he thought he saw a look of recognition on the mayor's face. But that was impossible, wasn't it? After all, he was dressed head to toe in fur.

But the way Mayor Guffey's lip curled...did she know it was him? Would the next words out of her mouth be...

"Yo! Sasquatch!" the cameraman repeated, intent on getting his sound bite. "What brings you to the festival?"

"The women!" Derek roared, and without hesitation, he threw his hairy arms around the mayor's neck and made exaggerated kissing noises to the delight of the crowd.

Mayor Guffey, never missing an opportunity to upstage, said loudly, "Oh, you better watch it. My boyfriend's a jealous man, and he owns a gun!"

Her entourage ate it up, and the mayor held on tight to Derek, not letting him leave.

"Folks, tell your friends, tell your neighbors—the Shakes-Beer Festival here in Fort Womack has something for everyone. From high brows to low brows..." she pointed at Derek, "to unibrows!"

Derek guffawed, slapping the mayor on the back.

"Now," Mayor Guffey said, ready to press on, "let's shoot over to the main stage. I've got a speech to give. Have fun, Mr. Bigfoot!"

Derek waved broadly as she departed, press in tow.

"Having fun?" Shelby asked.

"As a matter of fact—"

Derek didn't get a chance to finish his thought as a small drone buzzed overhead. It was painted in yellow and black stripes, and trailing behind was a banner that read, *Follow me to Mr. B!*

Shelby promptly took him by the arm.

"Come on. I think we've found Mr. Buckaroo."

Tom Buckaroo's booth was twice the size of the others around it. One half touted honey and beeswax products, and the other served up varieties of mead. A converted food truck sold Tom Buckaroo merchandise, and all the workers wore trademark tie-dyed shirts.

The drone came to roost next to one of the young workers. The kid swapped battery packs before sending it off on another run drumming up business.

"Where is he?" Shelby groused. "I don't see him."

"There," Derek said, pointing at a circle of women—some young, some old, all-in various levels of Shakespearean dress and all enraptured by the wiry-haired figure standing before them.

Tom Buckaroo was half Deadhead, half snake oil salesman, and at the moment, he was the center of attention. Derek recognized another huckster when he saw one, and Buckaroo was as slippery as they came. As they approached the short, middle-aged man wearing round glasses and Birkenstocks, Derek noticed that Tom's adoring fans were weighed down with purchases from his booth.

"Stop me if you've heard this one," Tom said, charming his audience. "Shakespeare walks into a bar. The bartender takes one look at him and says, 'Hey! You can't come in here. You're bard!' Get it? Now, who wants to buy my new Tom Buckaroo Body Scrub?"

His bevy of admirers couldn't get their credit cards out fast enough.

You've got to hand it to him. The man knows how to make a buck.

"Hey, Tom," Derek called, his voice muffled by the cumbersome mask.

Tom's gaze turned to the man in the hairy suit. "Egads, miladies! 'Tis a bear come to steal my honey!"

Derek sighed. "I am *not* a bear. I'm—"

Shelby stepped in front of Derek, sunlight glinting off her badge.

"Mr. Buckaroo, may we have a moment of your time?"

The crowd of customers took one look at the woman in uniform and scattered. Tom Buckaroo was left holding unsold jars of body scrub.

"This better be important," he said.

FOURTEEN

Rose gave a sigh of relief as they passed the Fort Womack city limits sign. Downtown was still a ways off, but at least the finish line was in sight. They'd be late, but they'd make it.

The gas gauge was well below empty by this point. Petalicious was going to have to up their game in the future. They'd have to rethink their supply chain, double-check all incoming orders, and keep at least one vehicle in prime working order at all times. Running on fumes was *not* her idea of a well-oiled machine.

She noticed that Daisy was rather quiet. Had she been too rough on her partner? Maybe it was just the unbearable heat. She snapped her fingers playfully.

"Hey, Daisy," Rose said. "You still with me?"

Daisy was staring out the window. To be specific, she was staring at her side mirror.

"That cloud is following us. It has been for a couple miles."

"What cloud?" Rose asked.

Daisy didn't reply. She just kept staring at the mirror. Rose tried to see what she was talking about, but the driver's side mirror was broken and only gave her a view of the road rushing past, and the rows of flowers blocked any view she might have gotten from the main rearview mirror.

"Next stop: downtown," Rose said. "Check that last email from the mayor's office and read off the location of the main stage, will you? Last year it was Carter Park, but I think they may have changed it to...Daisy? Are you listening to me?"

"It's getting lower."

"What is?"

"The cloud, damn it."

Rose craned her neck to try to see out of Daisy's mirror, but it was no use.

"Don't worry about it," Rose said, irked by Daisy's distraction. "The weather says clear skies for the rest of the weekend. I'm sure it will blow over—"

"It's dropping!"

"What the hell are you talking about?"

Daisy turned to her partner, pale as a lily. She tried to explain via hand signals, forming a V-shape in the air with her shaking hands.

"I don't know what you're trying to say," Rose said.

"Go faster."

"We're on empty, Daisy. You get the best gas mileage going fifty-five—"

"Go faster!" Daisy screamed.

A shadow crept over the Pilot's hood as the sun went AWOL. A second later, something rammed the back of the SUV.

Rose glanced up at the sunroof. Crawling over the glass

were scores of enormous bees, mandibles flexing, and sharp stingers leaving scratch marks.

Daisy screamed again, pointing at Rose's window. Rose whipped about and saw that a squadron of bees was pursuing them, wings beating so rapidly they were nothing but a blur, keeping pace with the SUV. Rose got a good look at the closest monster insect, and her skin crawled. Larger by far than a normal bee, it was proportioned a bit differently to make it aerodynamic. Its plump abdomen hung heavy, and its legs were much thicker, almost muscular. And its eyes, its multifaceted eyes—Rose could almost make out her reflection in their shiny surface.

"Rose!"

Rose turned front just in time to avoid hitting a motorcyclist. As the Pilot overtook the bike, so did the bees. Rose didn't witness the cyclist's fate, but she heard his vehicle explode under the barrage of bees.

A crack sounded overhead, and both women cried out, certain the sunroof was giving way. One of the bees had pierced the glass with its stinger, the barbed tip jabbing downward like a harpoon.

It was getting hard to see the road. Bees swarmed every surface of the vehicle. Another stinger pierced the glass, this time the passenger side window. Daisy leaned clear of the milky fluid running down the glass.

"Take this exit to Tremont Street," Rose's phone said.

Rose took the exit, and as she hit the straightaway toward downtown, her view of the road was swallowed up. All she could see were the underbellies of hundreds of bees, each and every one of them stabbing at the windshield with their stingers, intent on getting inside.

"Rose!" Daisy cried. "We've got to pull over."

"I know," Rose said.

"We're going to hit someone."

"I know!"

Rose hit the brakes. The wheels tried to lock, but the car kept on moving under the force of the swarm. The Pilot skidded, tires squealing as the SUV was dragged sideways down the street. Rose yanked on the wheel, and the vehicle swerved again—now they were speeding backward into town.

"Oh, God. I'm sorry," Rose said. "Daisy, I'm so, so sorry."

Daisy stared straight ahead. Then, she slowly slumped forward, cradled by her shoulder belt. Her head lolled to the side, and Rose spied the massive stinger lodged in her friend's right temple. The stinger's venom sac pulsed grotesquely. Daisy must have slammed against the window when the SUV swerved, impaling herself.

"Daisy?"

Rose grabbed the stinger and ripped it free. Milky venom dripped from her fingers, and an angry rash erupted on her palm. The rash spread quickly, up her forearm, across her chest, and up her neck.

Rose's jaw tightened, and she felt a cluster of pustules rise on her inner cheek. The blisters burst, flooding her mouth with pus. She tried to spit it out, but the majority of the warm liquid poured down her throat, cutting off her air, turning off the lights, and sending her body into spasm.

The SUV's tires left the ground as the swarm swept it up into its embrace. Rose felt her heart slow, and then she slipped into the same darkness into which Daisy had just tumbled, serenaded by the hum of countless wings.

FIFTEEN

"Where did you get this?"

Tom Buckaroo held the mason jar aloft, turning it slowly, examining the obscenely large bee in the from every angle.

"A couple of miles outside of town," Derek replied, surreptitiously raising his mask.

"Where *exactly?*"

"You should know. You sent a college kid my way. He was looking for an old topo map of yours."

Tom lowered the mason jar and threw a glance Shelby's way. "I don't know anything about any maps."

"Bullshit, Tom," Derek snapped.

"You're saying a kid was looking for *my* map but he came to *you* to find it?" Tom laughed. "That doesn't even make sense."

Derek could tell the man was sweating underneath his tie-dye shirt. What had gotten the fellow so riled? Was there something he didn't want Shelby to know?

Derek turned to Shelby.

"He sold me a bunch of props for the Odditorium. When we opened, it was looking a little sparse. For five hundred bucks, I bought ten boxes of crap from him to fill in the holes." He gave Tom a nasty look. "Emphasis on *crap.*"

"All right," Tom said. "I sold him some merchandise. But there were *no* maps."

"Some of them had your notes penciled on them."

"You calling me a liar? You, the man who brings me a fake bee to examine?" Tom shook the jar—the dead bee clunked about, losing a wing.

"Fake?" Derek fumed.

"First off, there are no bees this size. Never have been, never will be. Even *Megachile pluto*, also known as Wallace's giant bee, is only about four centimeters long. This thing? Ha! Even if it were real, I doubt it could even fly; it's so heavy."

"But I saw it fly," Shelby said.

Tom passed her the mason jar.

"My dear, you saw exactly what he wanted you to see. Manipulation is his bread and butter."

Derek looked over at Shelby. He could feel her allegiance shift.

"And here's a dead giveaway," Tom said, tapping on the glass. "You see this exoskeleton? It looks like it's forged out of metal. I'd say this is something he slapped together for that Odditorium of his."

"Tell her about the maps," Derek insisted.

"I don't know what you're talking about."

"Tell her! And while you're at it, tell her that *this...*" Derek held out the dead bee, "is the real deal."

Tom hooted with laughter.

"You're nuts, you know that?"

"Derek, let's let the man get back to his business," Shelby said, coaxing him away.

"No! He sold me the maps. And this bee is no fake! I swear to you on Molly's grave."

"I never got the chance to say my condolences, Derek," Tom said, hand over his heart. Then he whispered to Shelby. "Maybe that's why he's acting a little..." He circled his finger next to his temple—the international sign for "crazy."

Derek saw red. He launched himself at Tom Buckaroo, hairy, Squatchy hands grabbing the guy by his shirtfront. Tom squealed in fear.

"Are you going to tell her the truth or am I going to have to shake it out of you?" Derek shouted.

Tom tried to extract himself from the angry man's grasp but only managed to knock Derek's furry headpiece off.

"Get him off me! Officer! Help!"

Shelby set down the mason jar and inserted herself in between the fighting men. "Back off! Both of you."

Her intervention did the trick—Derek and Tom went to their corners seething. Derek glared at Tom. The man *definitely* had something to hide, otherwise, why was he being such a...

"Dick," a familiar voice behind him said, "will you look what we have here?"

"Looks like trouble to me, Chief."

Derek turned. Cross and one of his men stood, arms folded. They must have seen his dust-up with Tom. Chief Cross shook his head.

"Derek, Derek, Derek," he said, clucking his tongue. "You are dumber than a bag of hammers, you know that?"

"I...I..." Derek stammered.

"I guess you didn't hear me when I said the festival was off-limits."

"Sir, I can explain," Shelby said.

"No need, Officer. Looks pretty clear to me." Cross turned his attention to Tom. "And you, Mr. Buckaroo. Fighting in the streets?"

"He started it!"

"I don't care who started it. The mayor wants a peaceful festival, and a peaceful festival she's going to get. Dick, you take the bee man. I'll take..." Cross gave Derek and his costume the once-over. "Whatever *this* is supposed to be."

Derek found himself in one temporary holding cell; Tom was in another. The police had placed the cages along the west side of Johnson Park, which not only afforded the detainees a good view of the main stage but also the delightful experience of being downwind of the porta-potties.

Derek's "cage-mates" were a young man dressed in a toga who burped incessantly and an elderly woman who wouldn't stop glaring at him. Derek steered clear of them both. Tom, on the other hand, had a cage all to himself.

"This is going to cost me a fortune, you know that?" Tom grumbled.

"You've got plenty of worker bees to help sell your crap," Derek said.

"People come to see Tom Buckaroo!"

"Like that college kid did?"

Chief Cross approached with Shelby on his heels. Tom

shushed Derek, proving once again that, yes, the man had something he wanted to hide.

"I told you to keep him away," Cross said, addressing Shelby but looking at Derek.

Shelby grabbed his arm. "Sir, please—"

Cross threw off her hand. "Only person who touches me is my lady. Unless you want to share a cage with your brother-in-law, Officer Parker, I'd back the hell off."

Cross stalked off, leaving a stunned Shelby in his wake.

"Shelby!" Derek called. "You've got to get him to let me out of here."

"He's not going to listen to me."

"Make him."

Shelby threw up her hands. "And just how am I going to do that, Derek? The man's got it in for you, and now, thanks to your little scuffle, he's got *me* in his sights as well."

"Shelby..."

"I know, I know," Shelby said. "You swear on Molly's grave."

"I was going to say I'm sorry, but...yes, I do. I swear I'm telling the truth." Derek stared daggers at Tom. "About everything."

Shelby let out a half sigh/half moan. "I'll see what I can do. Don't go anywhere."

"Very funny."

She took off after Cross. Derek turned his attention back to Tom.

"Why are you lying?"

"I'm not! I—"

"It's just you and me here," Derek said. The young man in the toga burped again, undercutting Derek's point. "We both know that bee is real, and we both know the map that kid used was originally yours. Now...do you want to spill the beans, or are you going to keep lying like the gutless piece of trash you are?"

To Derek's surprise, Tom burst out laughing.

"Did I say something funny?"

"No, no," Tom said, still snickering. "It's just hard to take you seriously dressed like that."

Derek realized he still sported the bottom half of the Bigfoot costume. He wriggled out of the hairy pants and tossed them aside, leaving him in a T-shirt and shorts.

"Yes, of course the topo map was mine."

"Then, why—"

"Because the kid was looking for something that isn't quite...legal."

"Such as?"

Tom eyeballed the woman in the cage with Derek.

"I don't think she's a snitch." Derek turned to the elderly woman. "You're not a snitch, are you?" The woman just kept staring. "See? Not a snitch."

Tom pressed up against the bars of his cage and whispered, "Psychotropics."

"Huh?"

"Mind-altering plants," Tom reluctantly repeated. "You know...of the hallucinogenic persuasion."

Derek was having trouble putting two and two together. "But out where we saw the kid's van...there's nothing but grassland out there."

Tom grinned. "Maybe up top. But down below?"

The crevasse! Derek suddenly understood what the man was getting at.

"So, did you ever—"

"Nope. I'm strictly a mead man, myself," Tom said. "But I told the kid—who got the map from *you* after you got it from *me*—that its original owner, a hippy-dippy flower child from Ward, swore that she'd located a source back in the sixties using that map. For fifty bucks, I told the kid where he could find it."

"Which led him to me."

"In a nutshell."

"Lords and ladies," the PA system bellowed. *"I'd like to welcome to the stage the mayor of our fair city, the honorable Janice Guffey!"*

"As for that bee of yours," Tom said, "I need to get a better look at it. Up close, you know?"

Derek's attention was elsewhere. A dark cloud was rolling up Tremont Street toward the festival grounds. Derek caught his breath.

"Looks like you're about to get your wish."

SIXTEEN

Mayor Guffey pushed her wheelchair up to the microphone. She made a show of looking up at the mic—a couple of feet too tall to be of any use to her.

"I tried to tell them I don't do stand-up."

The audience roared.

A delinquent aide rushed over and adjusted the height.

"Sorry, ma'am."

"Thanks for the assist, Danny," the mayor said. "You can go clean out your desk now."

The audience roared at this as well. This was going to be an easy gig.

She cleared her throat, then launched into her spiel.

"Hello, ShakesBeerians!"

The audience cheered and raised their plastic cups.

"Welcome to the third annual ShakesBeer Festival, the premier beer and bard event this side of the Rocky Mountains!"

Self-congratulatory applause sounded all around.

"Now, I've had an opportunity to sample some of the

great beers our brewmasters have concocted for the occasion —A Winter's Ale, the Julius Saison, and one of my personal favorites, Exit, Pursued by a Beer—and I have to say, this year's selection is the best yet!"

A breeze tousled the mayor's hair.

Don't even think *about raining. I forbid it.*

"In addition to the libations, we have rustled up the finest acting talent the state has to offer. Where else can you sip Shakespearean cerveza while watching *Love's Labour's Lost?* Where else can you share a twelve-pack while taking in *Twelfth Night?* Does Boulder offer its people such a festival?"

The crowd responded with a resounding "No!"

"Does Aspen?"

"No!"

"Does Telluride?"

"NO!"

The mayor laughed. If only the citizenry were this agreeable and loaded the other 364 days of the year.

"That's right! Only here in Fort Womack! Now, let me introduce the man who's going to get this party started. The one, the only...Hamlet! Give it up for him. He's Danish!"

An actor dressed in a black cloak and tights bounded across the stage and took his place next to the mayor. He made a grand bow before Mayor Guffey. When he rose, he magically had a frosty mug in his right hand.

The crowd ate it up.

Hamlet took a big swig of ale, and wiped his mouth. He offered the mug to the mayor, who waved it off.

"Thank you, but no. I never drink and drive," she said, patting her wheelchair. "Hamlet, the stage is yours."

Hamlet stepped forward. He was a gangly fellow who spat when he spoke.

"Gentles all, let the revels begin! Grab yourselves an ale, a stout, a lager. *Romeo and Juliet* opens on the west stage, *Midsummer* on the east. And here on the main stage, I, Hamlet, shall be posing the eternal question, 'To be...'"

The actor paused for dramatic effect. As he did so, something landed on his head.

For a split second, Mayor Guffey thought a pigeon had just landed on the Prince of Denmark's head—Fort Womack was lousy with the filthy beasts. But the longer she looked, the more she realized it was no pigeon. It was a bee the size of a rotisserie chicken.

Hamlet was too stunned to move. Then, despite the giant insect clinging to his head, the actor's reflexes kicked in—the show had to go on, didn't it?

"Or not to be," he finished.

A collective scream rose from the crowd. The mayor whirled her chair about, trying to locate the reason for the outburst. It wasn't hard to do. Tearing its way up Tremont Street was a funnel cloud made of bees, revelers scattering in terror before it.

As if that weren't enough, an SUV suddenly plummeted from the sky and landed directly behind the main stage in an explosion of smoke and flowers. Mangled lilies fell at the mayor's feet.

"Holy shit," Mayor Guffey gasped.

SEVENTEEN

P anic gripped the fairgoers as the massive column of bees approached. The insects were locked in formation once again, a massive spinning top smashing everything in its path. The furious swarm upended tables filled with merchandise and tossed revelers aside like rag dolls. It swallowed up kiosks, bicycles, and picnic tables galore. A debris field of splintered wood and broken glass orbited the base of the bee tornado, sending sharp projectiles slamming into storefronts and shoppers alike.

The sound of the approaching swarm was the stuff of nightmares. Derek had heard tornados before in all their rumbling glory. This was something quite different. The funnel roared like a giant monster from a Saturday night creature feature show.

"Tom!" Derek shouted over the din. "You're the expert. What do we do?"

Tom Buckaroo was busy examining the wire mesh that made up his detention cell.

"Tom!"

"They're too big to get inside these cages, but…"

"But what?"

"But I don't think that's going to matter."

As if to prove Tom's point, a screaming hot dog vendor and his cart were sucked up into the swarm.

The churning behemoth was closing fast. Detritus spewed from its top, spraying in all directions. Nothing escaped its wrath. Not trees, not vehicles, not drunken actors standing in its way.

"Blow, winds, and crack your cheeks! Rage! Blow! You cataracts and hurricanoes…" cried an old thespian, staff in one hand and a flagon of ale in the other. Derek averted his eyes as the tempest consumed the man.

Tom was frantically removing his belt.

"What the hell are you doing?" Derek cried.

"Lashing myself to one of these walls," Tom answered as he looped his belt through the wire mesh. "In a few seconds, we're going to be bouncing around inside these things like balls in a bingo ball cage. I, for one, don't want my head cracked open!"

Derek quickly looked at his two cage-mates. The elderly woman must have been listening to Tom's explanation as she was already tying herself to the side of the cell with a floral scarf.

Derek knelt before the burping toga kid. The boy was passed out. He ripped off the young man's sheet, hoping he'd be wearing something else beneath. Unfortunately, he was not.

Derek made quick work tying one corner of the makeshift toga to the cage wall. He yanked the toga kid to his feet, tucked them both inside like it was bedtime, and secured the opposite sheet corner. It wasn't the tightest tethering, but it would have to...

And then the bee tornado was on top of them.

The first wave of insects slammed against Derek's cage, tipping it precariously. The young man in the sheet with Derek stirred but didn't wake.

His blood alcohol level must be through the roof.

The base of the twister was upon them. The cloud of insects carried an odd scent—equal parts floral and metallic. The deep reverberation of the buzzing choir made Derek's eardrums vibrate like crazy. The light faded as the flying monstrosities engulfed the cage.

Derek's distress was off the charts. He tried desperately to think of the swarm as a single entity, but that was impossible as he clearly saw individual bees clinging to the sides of the cage. His childhood fear welled up inside, threatening to spill out. It probably would have, had the young man cradled in the sheet with him not roused.

"Holy crap!" the man cried and threw his arms around Derek's neck.

Derek felt the cage shift. It made a jerky one-eighty, then tipped slowly onto its side. Derek found himself dangling as the wall he'd just tied himself to became the new ceiling.

Toga guy clung about Derek's neck like a drowning man. Derek quickly found it difficult to breathe.

"Dude, let go!" he wheezed. "Grab hold of the sheet instead!"

But having awakened to a buzzing nightmare, the guy was in no frame of mind to listen. Instead, he clawed desperately at Derek's face. Derek tried to wrap an arm around the man's chest to pull him in close, but the fellow threw him off, toppling out of the sheet cocoon.

The next wave hit, tossing the cages like dice. Derek held on for dear life as the enclosure tumbled through the park, buffeted by the swarm. Untethered as he was, the young man tumbled about the cage. Derek tried to catch the poor guy, but it was no use. The young man was, as Tom had put it, a ball in a bingo cage.

The world had gone topsy-turvy. Derek was viewing it from inside a clothes dryer. He fought to remain conscious though the darkness beckoned.

The joyride came to an abrupt halt as the cage slammed into one of the park's enormous Ponderosa pines. The cage groaned under the pressure of the bees' assault. Its sides began to buckle, the metal molding itself around the tree trunk like it was made of aluminum foil.

We're going to be crushed inside this damn cage!

Steel groaned as the cell compressed. Rivets popped, and the wall to which the elderly woman was lashed ripped free. Derek locked eyes with her a moment before an upswell of insects lifted her into the air. The woman let loose a scream as she disappeared into the funnel.

Toga guy struggled to hold onto the cage. Derek reached out a hand.

"Here!"

It was no use. One second, the man was there; the next, he was hurtling upward, vacuumed up into the buzzing vortex.

Derek was alone, trapped inside the remains of the holding cell. The raging swarm pressed hard against the cage, crushing him between the wire mesh and the tree trunk like trash in a compactor. Derek closed his eyes, preparing for the worst.

Suddenly the pressure eased. The funnel was collapsing, bees abandoning their adopted form. They veered off in a swirling cloud, circling the park, Derek and the rest of the fairgoers caught in the eye of their storm.

Derek tried to pry himself loose from the twisted metal, but it held firm. With much effort, he managed to work one of his knees to his chest and planted his foot firmly in the center of the panel. Straining with the effort, Derek pressed the heavy panel with all his might until, finally, he wrenched it free from the tree. The panel toppled to the ground. Derek was not far behind.

He groaned as he landed, temporarily dazed, the wind knocked out of him.

Come on, get up, get up...

As Derek stood, his heart sank as he surveyed the aftermath surrounding him. Fort Womack's downtown, which had been perfectly bucolic not moments ago, had been reduced to a scene straight out of a postapocalyptic nightmare. Most of the booths were flattened, and some had disappeared completely. How many people had been injured or simply swept away? He dared not speculate.

A bronze statue had stopped Tom's cage in its tracks, a frontiersman's rifle coming dangerously close to running the old boy clean through. He was still lashed to the cage.

"You okay?" Derek called.

"Shook up but still here," Tom moaned.

"What the hell are they doing?" Derek asked, nodding toward the sky. "It looks like they're circling us."

"They are."

"Why?"

"Why does any predator circle its prey? They're looking for their next point of attack."

Derek carefully picked his way over to Tom's cage. The wails of sirens mixed with those of the injured. Derek's thoughts turned to Mel, and his hand went for his phone. Gone, taken by one of Cross's men. He and the chief would have words when they next met, he assured himself.

"You want to get me out of here?"

Tom's voice snapped Derek back to the present.

"Sorry," Derek said. "Picking locks isn't in my skill set."

"I wasn't talking to you."

Derek turned. Shelby was standing behind him. She looked like she'd seen her own share of the action. Her uniform was torn, and her customarily pulled-back hair hung loose.

She held an ornate battle axe in her hand, its blade dripping with bee goo.

"Stand back," she said.

EIGHTEEN

Derek stood anxiously by as Shelby hacked away at Tom's cage with the axe. His head was still spinning. It would be easy to give in to panic, but he wasn't about to take that road. He tried to put aside the image of the young man disappearing into the swarm but failed miserably.

"Come on!" Shelby snarled, striking the cell door once more. *Whack!* She was strong, but the cage was stronger.

"Where'd you get that?" Derek was impressed with the way his sister-in-law handled the hefty weapon.

"Confiscation tent. You wouldn't believe what people bring to this festival. Swords, maces, shields." *Whack!*

"You didn't happen to grab my phone in the process? Cross took mine when he stuck me in his cage," Derek said. "I need to check on Mel."

"No," Shelby said, scowling at him. "I was kind of busy saving myself from those damn bees of yours."

"Oh, now that you believe me, they're *my* bees."

"Fine. Use mine."

Shelby held out her phone. Derek grabbed it and dialed Mel's number. His daughter's phone rang and rang and rang.

Damn it, Mel. Pick up.

"You want to spell me?"

Derek looked up. Shelby held out the axe. She looked spent.

He traded her the phone for the axe, which was a lot heavier than he'd expected. Luckily, Shelby had made good headway, and it only took a half dozen strikes before the lock gave way. The job complete, Derek passed the axe back to Shelby.

Tom Buckaroo stumbled out of his cell. Gone was his bravado—in its place, an ever-rising panic.

"They're stalking us," Tom said, staring up at the circling swarm.

"Why?" Shelby asked. "What did *we* do to them?"

"We're giving off alarm pheromones. You, me, everyone in this park."

"What can we do about that?" Derek asked.

"Run."

Derek flinched—his mother's imperative coming out of the man's mouth.

Shelby wasted no time. She was off like a shot, striding across the fairgrounds.

"What are you doing?" Derek called, following at her heels.

"I'm making a beeline to the station," Shelby said. "Pun intended. The expert said run; I'm running."

Tom hurried to catch up with them. "What's the plan?"

"There's a bomb shelter in the basement at the station, not to mention guns galore."

Tom shook his head emphatically. "We'll be easy pickings if we try to make it there on foot. My booth is only a stone's throw away. I have a food truck that could survive Armageddon. Safer to drive to the station. Agreed?"

Shelby stopped in place and turned to Derek.

"What do you think?"

"I like his plan," Derek said emphatically. "Good plan."

"Fine."

Shelby motioned for Tom to proceed.

"Lead on, Macduff."

As the trio forged ahead, they passed more evidence of the bees' awesome destructive power. One-on-one, the monster insects were frightening enough; swarming together, they were downright terrifying. Trees lay uprooted and porta-potties littered the park. A young woman screamed her dog's name over and over. In one of the few miracles of that day, her little rat terrier suddenly appeared, crawling out from under a crushed face painting booth.

"Lulu!" the woman cried as the pooch leaped into her arms, covering her in bright paint and glitter.

The bees continued to circle Johnson Park like jets awaiting the go-ahead signal from air traffic control. Derek had no interest in being out in the open when they began their descent.

Tom paused to kneel before a dead bee lying amongst the litter, its legs curled up in death. He grabbed up a stick and poked at a dead bee.

"Quick. I need something to put this in."

Trash cans upended in the melee had strewn their contents far and wide. Derek spotted a plastic bag rolling with the wind like a tumbleweed and snagged it before it could escape. He handed the bag to Tom, who gently eased the oversized insect into it.

"My truck is up ahead," Tom called, rising and picking up the pace.

Tom's vehicle, a modified food truck with Tom Buckaroo products listed on its side, stood intact, service window down and secured. Tom's booth, on the other hand, was ripped to shreds. A lone employee stood amidst the ruins, trying to salvage what he could from the scattered merchandise.

"Billy!" Tom called. "Don't worry about that."

"But, Mr. Buckaroo...the booth...the bees..." The pimple-faced kid was near tears.

"The only thing that matters is that you're okay," Tom said, clapping the kid on the back. "What about the others? Josie? Koko?"

"They ran. I stayed and tried to..." Now the kid *did* cry. Tom gave the boy a hug.

"Don't worry," Tom said, throwing open the truck's back door. "Come with us, son. We're getting the hell out of here."

"Yes, sir. Thank you, sir."

Billy didn't need to be told twice. He immediately scrambled into the truck.

Shelby's phone rang. She checked the number.

"Derek, it's Mel."

"Finally!" Derek held out his hand.

Shelby tossed him the phone.

"Be right with you," he said to Tom.

"Make it quick," Tom warned, ushering Shelby into the truck.

Derek answered the call.

"Dad? Why are you using Aunt Shelby's phone?"

"Never mind. Are you okay?"

There was a pause on the other end of the line.

"Mel, are you okay?"

"Yeah..."

"Good. Well, I'm okay. Aunt Shelby is okay."

"Okay."

Derek didn't want to scare the girl, but he needed to make sure she was safe until he got back home.

"Listen, you know the Tommyknockers display in the Odditorium? That's the one with—"

"Yeah, Dad, I know it."

"Inside the Tommyknocker's cave, there's a trapdoor in the floor. Open it, and there's a ladder that leads down into a crawlspace. That's where the smoke machine is. If you see *anything* out of the ordinary, I want you to go down into the crawlspace until I get home."

"Why?"

"Promise me, Melissa."

Shelby's phone crackled with static. Derek thought he heard Mel reply in the affirmative, but he couldn't be sure.

Then the line went dead.

Derek tried Mel's number again, but all he got was an electronic warbling sound. Hopefully, he'd gotten his message across loud and clear.

He turned back toward the truck and, in doing so, stepped directly into a puddle. Derek sighed. He was ankle-deep in a pool of Tom Buckaroo's famous barrel-aged mead. The barrel was nowhere in sight.

Clean up on aisle three, he thought ruefully.

Derek was in the process of shaking out his sopping shoe when a humming sound stopped him cold.

Crouched before him, sipping away at the spilled mead, was a bee the size of Lulu, the rat terrier.

"Oh boy," Derek whispered.

NINETEEN

Derek stared at the bee as it lapped up the mead. Until that very minute, he had no idea bees even had tongues. He'd have to confirm that with Tom if he managed to make it to the safety of the food truck.

A second bee descended lazily from above, joining its fellow hive mate at the pool, lured by the scent of the sweet liquid. A third joined them, followed by a fourth and a fifth. In short order, half a dozen of the things had gathered to feed on the spilled mead.

If Tom's stuff was this much of a draw, how long would it be before the whole swarm paid a visit?

Derek stood stock still. Taken as a group, he'd found the bees manageable, phobia-wise. But standing in the open with six of the humming monstrosities practically at his feet was proving to be too much. The familiar fear began tickling his brain. His fight-or-flight impulse demanded he make a choice, and he responded loud and clear: *flight, flight, flight!*

One of the bees took the initiative to crawl closer. It was only natural, as the far side of the pool had become quite crowded—a humming happy hour. As it approached, wending its way toward Derek, a voice in his head screamed, *It's coming to get you! Run!*

Derek's legs moved before he gave them the order. The sudden movement threw him off balance, and despite his frantic efforts to remain vertical, Derek stumbled backward, landing on his butt in the middle of Lake Mead.

Undeterred by his fall, the industrious bee kept coming. And when it reached Derek's mead-soaked leg, it crawled right on up.

You should have run.

"Stratton!"

You should have RUN!

"Derek!"

The urgency in Tom's voice was enough to get Derek to raise his head. Staring past the encroaching bee—*it's on my thigh*—he spotted Tom hanging out of the back of his food truck.

"Hold your breath."

The bee inched its way across his belly.

"What?" Derek said in a voice below a whisper.

"They're attracted to carbon dioxide. Hold..."

The bee scampered up his chest.

"...your..."

A tentative leg touched his throat.

"...breath!"

A second before the insect crawled onto his face, Derek obeyed and took a breath. He knew he'd have to let it out eventually, but at present, he was determined to outlast a deep-sea diver.

The bee examined his every feature. It dropped his

proboscis and tickled his lips. It stared down at its own reflection in his tear-filled eyes. But when it brushed a bristly leg against his nose, Derek couldn't hold out any longer. His diaphragm clenched. A sneeze was coming despite all his efforts to squelch it.

This is it, Derek thought, as he loosed the sneeze that would surely end him. A blast of air erupted from his nose and mouth.

The bees reacted as one. They rose like a squadron of helicopters. The bee on his face—having been blown free by the force of the sneeze—returned with a fury. Derek saw the thing's stinger poised and ready to plunge.

The next moment, he was coughing on smoke.

"Get to the truck!" It was Tom's voice, though he couldn't see the man through the thick cloud.

Derek did as commanded, bees be damned. He hurried to his feet, got his directional bearings, and ran for the food truck. Shelby hung out the back, arm extended.

"Grab my hand," she ordered.

Derek was all too happy to obey. He made a dive for her hand, missed it, doubled back and made an ungraceful leap for the door. His knees screamed as they hit the bumper, but Billy and Shelby were there and ready to pull him aboard. He toppled into a stack of cardboard boxes with a *crunch.*

"Where's Mr. Buckaroo?" Billy asked.

"I'm here, I'm here," Tom coughed. He had Shelby's pilfered battle axe in one hand, a working bee smoker in the other. He tossed both aside, grabbed the handholds on either side of the door, and hoisted himself inside.

"Close that door!" he cried, stumbling over the prone Derek to get to the driver's seat.

Billy shut the door, Tom started up the engine, and they were off, Tom Buckaroo merchandise clattering off shelves.

Shelby gave Derek a hand up.

"Do you know where you're going?" she called to Tom.

"Do I look like someone who doesn't know where the local constabulary is stationed?"

"Just making sure."

The food truck hit a ditch, and Shelby stumbled. Derek caught her before she could fall.

"Thanks," she said under her breath.

"Don't mention it."

"Uh...Mr. Buckaroo?" It was Billy.

"What?"

"I think we're leaking."

Derek went over to the boy. "What do you mean, leaking?"

Billy looked down. Derek followed his gaze. He had noticed when he was on the floor that it was a bit wet—now he understood why.

The boxes he landed on as he'd vaulted into the truck were labeled *Mead–Gold Reserve*. The thick, sticky liquid flowed out from inside one of them, spread across the floor, and seeped through the gap at the bottom of the back door.

Derek pushed Billy aside and stared out the rear window. A swirl of giant bees followed them, growing in number with every passing second, drawing the rest of the swarm out of the sky.

"Tom!"

"What now?"

"The kid's right. We're leaking mead out the back."

"So?"

"Tom...they're on our tail."

The old fellow looked back just in time to catch a bee landing on the rear window, blotting out the view.

"Son of a gun!"

Tom tried shaking the bee loose, giving the wheel a quick back and forth, but only succeeded in throwing his passengers off balance.

"Easy there, Buckaroo!" Derek shouted.

"Sorry!"

"Hey!" Shelby made her way up to Tom. "We're passing the station."

Tom didn't answer. He just gave the truck more gas.

Shelby leaned in. Derek thought she was about to take control of the wheel.

"Let us out!"

"I can't," Tom replied, the truck plowing through a banner for *Titus Andronicus.*

"Like hell you can't!"

"If I stop here, they'll swarm the station, and then where are we?" Tom yelled, swerving to dislodge the banner. "Tell the others to get ready to jump."

"Are you crazy?"

"I've been accused of that very thing. Get back there and get ready to jump. Trust me!"

Derek turned to Billy. "You got the door?"

The kid grabbed for the handle. Derek stopped his hand.

"Let's wait for the boss's signal, okay?"

"Okay," Billy agreed.

"Get ready, folks," Tom said. "One..."

Shelby joined Derek and Billy at the back door.

"Does he know what he's doing?" she asked, wild-eyed.

"I have no idea," Derek said.

"Two…"

Billy braced himself. Derek flashed Tom a thumbs-up. Whether or not the old guy saw him was anybody's guess.

"Three! Go, go, go!"

Billy threw the door open, and the three of them leaped like paratroopers executing a combat jump. The ground below was a blur, and when Derek hit, he felt the rush of bees swooping overhead. He landed hard and unsuccessfully tried to control his roll. Instead, he flailed as he tumbled, coming to an abrupt stop when he slammed into a trash can. Garbage and his wits went flying.

He rolled painfully to the side, extracting himself from the trash, and found Shelby and Billy not far off, both having had their own misadventures after exiting the truck. Billy was embedded in a shrub, and Shelby lay amongst the shattered remains of a ticket booth.

He whipped about when he heard the food truck's horn blasting the old Jimmie Rodgers hit, "Honeycomb." The swarm had dipped down from the sky like a great eel. And it had Tom's truck in its jaws.

"Come on," Derek cried out. "Come on, Tom. Jump! Jump!"

The tsunami of bees engulfed the truck, lifting it off its wheels. A moment before it disappeared in the upswell of insects, Derek spotted a figure exit the vehicle and tumble downward. From where he sat, Tom Buckaroo had just taken a good twenty-foot fall.

The bees, for their part, took to the skies with their prize.

Derek thought he could still hear the truck blasting the golden oldie as it disappeared with the swarm.

Derek was about to get up when a foot pressed him back down. He glanced up. Silhouetted in the sunlight stood Chief Cross, standing over him like a force of nature.

"The mayor would like a word."

TWENTY

Derek and Tom sat in the chief's office as Shelby conferred with her colleagues out in the bullpen. The station was abuzz with activity—phones rang off the hook, and radios squawked. The place was a model of organized chaos.

Derek tapped his feet like a student waiting for the principal to arrive. Tom was busy checking out the bee in the plastic bag.

"I see you held onto it," Derek said.

Tom didn't answer. He just kept rolling the bee about in the bag.

"You don't look any worse for the wear."

"What's that?" Tom asked, oblivious to everything but the bee's corpse.

"A fall like that might have taken a lesser man out of the game."

"Oh, well...luckily, I'm not a lesser man," Tom replied. He looked around as if just noticing where he was. "You didn't happen to see where they took Billy, did you?"

"They let him go after they took his statement. The kid looked pretty eager to leave. I think you're going to have to find yourself some new employees."

"And a new truck." Tom held out the bee in the bag. "These bees? They aren't your ordinary *Apis mellifera*. First off, they're freaking huge. Then there's the pollen."

"What about it?"

Tom ran a finger along one of the bee's legs. "Get the light."

Derek flicked the light switch, and the office dimmed.

"See?"

Tom rubbed his fingers together. The dusty pollen gave off a phosphorescent glow.

"Mother Nature had herself some fun back in prehistoric days. She grew bees big. Blocked out the sun with ash, forcing flowers to adapt or die. Hmm..."

"What?"

Tom shook his hand. "It tingles."

"So, the bees and the flowers...you're saying they're prehistoric?"

"I am."

"Then what the hell are they doing here?"

"That's what I'd like to know," Mayor Guffey said, flipping on the light and pushing past them in her chair. Chief Cross entered behind her and leaned against the wall, affording the mayor the use of his desk as well as giving him a good spot from which to keep his eye on Derek.

Shelby slipped into the room and stood silently. She had the look of a kid who'd been taken out to the woodshed.

The mayor leaned across the desk toward Derek.

"Earlier today, you made a scene about giant killer bees—"

"And you wouldn't listen," Derek objected.

"You made a scene," the mayor continued, "and now here we are. Smack dab in the middle of a public safety emergency. I want to know everything that you know. What they are, where they came from, how we get rid of them."

Tom let loose an involuntary laugh.

"Did I say something funny, Mr. Buckaroo?"

"No, ma'am," Tom said. "That's just a typical bureaucrat's response. 'What is it and how do we kill it?'"

"I'd say that's the only responsible response to have. Citizens have been attacked, the festival's been shot to shit." She turned to the chief. "Do we have a number of the injured yet?"

"That info's still coming in," Cross replied. "It's going to be up there."

"You see?" Mayor Guffey pounded the desk, making everyone jump. "So you'll forgive me for being a typical bureaucrat, Mr. Buckaroo."

"What do you need to know?" Derek offered, ready to pass the weight of this nightmare onto another's shoulders.

Mayor Guffey folded her hands. "Now, we're getting somewhere."

The phone on the chief's desk rang. Perturbed at the interruption, Cross shouted out the doorway, "Who is it?"

"Sounds important, Chief," a voice from the bullpen called. "He wants to talk to you *and* the mayor."

The mayor and the chief shared a glance, then Mayor Guffey answered the call, putting it on speaker.

"Mayor Guffey. Who's this?"

The line cracked, then was replaced by a rhythmic *whump-whump* sound that Derek recognized: the spinning blades of a helicopter.

"Howdy, Mayor. Jim Mix, here. I understand you've got yourselves a big hullabaloo down there."

Big Jim Mix.

Derek realized he shouldn't be surprised, but he was, nonetheless.

"I don't know where you heard that, Mr. Mix, but we've got things under control."

"Word travels fast, Madam Mayor. I make it my business to stay apprised, especially where twisters are concerned."

The mayor punched the mute button.

"Who the hell am I talking to?" she demanded of the room.

"That's Jim Mix," Cross replied. "He's got that show on TV. He's legit."

Derek had to bite his tongue. Jim Mix legit? That was like saying the National Enquirer deserved the Pulitzer Prize in journalism.

The mayor unmuted the phone.

"I think you've been misinformed, Mr. Mix. What we've got here is a unique situation."

"What you've *got* is a damn bee tornado, yes, I know. Ain't that a kick in the head? That's why I'm making a stopover to pick up a friend of mine over at Rock U. An expert in the little critters. Twixt him and me, we're gonna sort out this mess for you, comprende?"

"Rocky Mountain University?" Tom whispered to Derek. "He can't mean Jefferson Gale, that hack!"

"Thank you for your concern, Mr. Mix," the mayor said, "but I already have a call in to the National Guard—"

"I know. Fellow who took your call, Col. Cheever, is a dear friend of mine. Says he'll let me have first crack at this, if you're agreeable."

"Why should I be?"

"Because I'm gonna save that little town of yours and your reputation. You let the National Guard in, they'll take all the credit. You let me in, I'll let you be the hero. All I want is unlimited access for my TV crew. What do you say, Mayor?"

The mayor muted the call once more.

"Get them out of here," she ordered, nodding at Derek and Tom.

Tom stood.

"I must protest. The man Mr. Mix is proposing to bring on knows as much about bees as I do about riding a unicycle, which is *nothing*. I don't know *anything* about riding a unicycle."

Mayor Guffey waved him off and resumed the call as the chief escorted everyone out of the room.

Shelby procured a replacement radio before approaching Cross. "Are they free to go?"

The chief looked Derek up and down. "We've got bigger fish to fry. Get him out of here."

Derek didn't budge. "Any chance I can get my phone back?"

"Martin!" Cross barked to a uniformed officer. "Get these men their belongings. Mr. Stratton has a property to vacate."

The street outside the station was awash with fairgoers seeking safety and first responders tending to the injured. Shelby pulled Derek and Tom away from the crowd.

"This fellow Mix, has he handled anything like this before?"

Tom laughed sarcastically. "There's never been anything like this before."

"Damn it!" Derek pocketed his phone.

"What's wrong, Derek?" Shelby asked.

"It's Mel," Derek said, his brow furrowed. "She's not picking up. You'd better take me home. I need to check on her."

"What?" Tom cried. "And leave Mix and his people to muck this situation up worse than it already is?"

"Tom..."

"You came to me, right? We need to move on this. *Now.* We are the only ones who know what the bees are after," Tom continued, holding up the plastic bag.

"We do?" Shelby asked.

"Those kids went looking for some type of flower, the same type these bees have been feeding on."

An ambulance blasted its siren, and the trio stepped out of its path.

"What are you getting at?" Shelby demanded.

"You've dealt with junkies before, I assume," Tom said. "What happens when they go cold turkey?"

"They get pretty pissed off," Shelby said, recognition spreading across her face.

"Just like our friends, the bees."

Shelby almost jumped out of her skin. "So, if we can get our hands on some of those flowers..."

Tom grinned.

"We'll have some damn powerful bait."

"He makes a good argument," Shelby admitted.

"And what about my daughter?" Derek was getting heated. "For all I know, she's hunkered down in a musty old crawlspace, scared out of her wits."

Shelby looked from Derek to Tom, then pulled her phone and dialed.

"Honey, I need a favor. Need you to check in on my niece over at my sister's place, can you do that?" She gave the address, then flashed the guys a thumbs-up. "Thanks. Love you too."

She pocketed her phone and held out her hands as if she had just performed a magic trick.

"Justine's heading over to your place right now. Satisfied?"

Derek nodded grudgingly.

"Great!" Tom bellowed. "Let's gear up."

TWENTY-ONE

Derek felt a tickle of jealousy as Shelby pulled the cruiser into the parking lot at Tom Buckaroo's Bee Farm and Honey Depot. The place was closed for the day due to the festival, but he could easily imagine the sizable crowds that the guy must attract. The Odditorium was charming in a garish, homemade sort of way, but it paled in comparison to the slick outfit Tom was running here on the outskirts of town.

"Nice setup," Derek said.

"We make do," Tom replied.

The main building was a geodesic dome painted to look like a beehive. It made for an impressive picture with the snowcapped Rockies in the background. Tom Buckaroo-branded signs directed customers to the retail store, the tasting room, and Buckaroo's Bee Trail, a maze snaking through fields of wildflowers. There was even a small outbuilding catering to any stings visitors might receive, aptly named The Ouch House.

"Take the service drive around to the left," Tom said,

riding shotgun. "My workshop is two klicks north."

Shelby turned off the dirt road, kicking up clouds of dust in the process. Derek, who had the privilege of sitting in the back seat, got a mouthful of grit.

"Close your window, will you, Shelby?" Derek coughed.

"Sorry."

Up ahead lay an older structure, formerly a barn from the looks of it. Tom had added some modern features, such as solar panels on the roof and sleek board-and-batten siding.

"Why are these bees acting like a tornado?" Shelby asked.

"A couple of possibilities come to mind," Tom mused. "When it comes to your garden variety honeybees, a so-called bee tornado is a protective mechanism."

"Protective?" Derek asked. "What are they protecting?"

"The queen, of course. When she goes looking for a new location for a hive, the colony will swarm about her. Confuses predators, you know? Anyway, some folks call it a bee tornado, some call it a bee cyclone. It's usually harmless behavior, unless—"

"Unless the bees are the size of bulldogs," Shelby said.

"Bingo."

"You think that's what's happening?" Derek asked. "They're guarding the queen?"

"Not so fast," Tom said, wagging a finger. "Bees are *also* hardwired to take orders. Like the military. And now that the swarm is going through some heavy-duty withdrawal, they're itching for some sort of structure. Along comes a twister and...*tada!* They have one hell of a pattern to latch onto." He undid his seatbelt. "Just park anywhere."

As well-manicured as the barn was on the outside, the interior was more akin to the chaos Derek was used to. A couple of workstations for hive repair, a candle-making setup, and plenty of boxes piled high with copper tubing, scraps of lumber, jars and bottles of various sizes.

"Welcome to my laboratory," Tom said in his best Bela Lugosi voice.

"I thought Frankenstein was the one with the lab," Derek said, peering into a barrel filled to the brim with assorted hardware.

"You're right," Tom said, nodding. "Always get those two mixed up."

Tom rattled off a list of items he was looking for, and the three of them set about procuring them. Bungee cords, rope, newspaper, five-gallon buckets. The three scurried about the barn until the final things on Tom's list had been gathered.

"What the hell is this?" Shelby asked, uncovering a steel keg with a picture of a scantily-clad woman in a bee costume slapped on the side.

"Ahh...that," Tom said, rushing to her side. "Sometimes groups rent out the farm to hold their events. Weddings, bar mitzvahs, you name it."

"This certainly doesn't look like something you'd trundle out for a child's birthday party."

"True, true! You see, we've just started hosting bachelor parties as well. This specialized tap I've invented allows the user—the bachelor, in this case—to shower another person in mead via this wand." He held up what looked like a pressure washer's business end and squeezed the trigger. Golden mead burst forth from the showerhead and splattered on the floor. "Of course, we use fresh mead on the day."

"Shower another person?" Shelby asked, rolling her eyes. "Such as a stripper?"

Tom shrugged. "Hey, give the customer what they want, right?"

"That's disgusting."

"That's commerce."

"Let's keep this moving, shall we?" Derek said, trying to spur the old fellow on.

"Sure thing. And now," Tom said, extracting a piece of equipment from atop a storage shelf filled with junk, "the pièce de résistance."

What Derek had first mistaken as a child's toy turned out to be a twin to the drone he and Shelby had followed to Tom's booth when the festival was still a festival, not a battle zone. Tom switched the little craft on and steered it through the air to where Shelby stood.

"What do you use this for? Looking down women's shirts?" she asked.

Tom held up the remote, which looked like an elaborate video game controller. "This Bogie 99-G is equipped with a camera, floodlight, and, best of all, an extendable arm for the ol' snatch-and-grab!"

"What does it snatch and grab?" Shelby asked. Her estimation of Tom had obviously dropped a peg or two.

A small utility arm lowered from the drone's underbelly and grabbed for the cord in Shelby's hand. She gently batted the drone away.

"A couple of trips underground, and we should have enough flowers to grab the swarm's attention," Tom said, landing the drone at his feet.

Derek had to admit it was a little bit of genius on Tom's part. Having viewed the crevasse up close and personal, he didn't relish the idea of crawling down the same hole that had birthed the bees.

"So we gather the bait, and then what?" Shelby asked. She had skepticism written all over her face. "We wait around twiddling our thumbs, hoping they'll catch a whiff?"

"Actually, you're not too far off," Tom said, setting the remote aside. "A bee's sense of smell is over one hundred times greater than ours. They can sniff out a patch of flowers from miles away. Miles, imagine that! We gather our rosebuds, so to speak, aerosolize them, and whammo! We won't be able to keep them away."

Shelby turned to Derek. "And I thought *you* were the craziest person in Butte County."

"So," Derek said, urging Tom on, "let's say we manage to lure the bees to us. Then what?"

"We're all on the same page here, correct?" Tom asked, staring pointedly at Shelby. "I mean, we all want these bees out of the picture."

"Why are you looking at me?" Shelby asked, eyes narrowing.

"Because we need *one* last item that your, shall we say, more *lawful* side might take issue with."

"Don't tell me you've got a bazooka hidden in here."

Tom laughed. "Nothing of the sort."

He stepped away for a brief moment, and when he returned, he was pushing a red metal container the size of a small safe.

"That's a storage magazine," Shelby said, her interest piqued.

"It is."

"What's it for?" Derek asked.

"Why, to store my dynamite in, what else?" Tom turned

to Shelby. "And before you ask, no, I do not have a permit to own it, store it, or use it. But I'm showing it to you, nonetheless."

Shelby's eyes flicked back and forth between Tom and the container. Derek half expected his sister-in-law to put the man in cuffs right then and there, but she surprised him with what she said next.

"Do you know how to handle it?"

"Been busting up tree stumps with it for over thirty years. Funny thing is that's how I got into the bee business. I blasted the hell out of a stubborn cottonwood stump only to find out that a colony had taken up residence. I must have been stung a couple of dozen times that day, but it got me thinking. One year later, Tom Buckaroo's Bee Farm was born."

"Hold on...what do we need dynamite for?" Derek asked. "Do you expect us to blast them out of the sky?"

"God, no. Besides, I found out the hard way that when dynamite explodes, it releases carbon dioxide. Maybe that's why the little buggers were so eager to get a taste of me."

Derek was growing frustrated—why wouldn't the guy just jump to the chase?

"If you have a plan, illuminate us, will you? Time's not a luxury we have right now."

Tom grew instantly serious. "The man Mix is bringing in? Jefferson Gale? What the man lacks in apian expertise, he makes up for in cruelty. You want to know my plan? I want to lure those bees—who were never meant to survive in the modern world—back into that crevasse and seal it off. Gale? His plan will no doubt involve something more sinister."

"Like what?" Derek asked.

"Like blasting them out of the sky."

"Fine by me," Shelby said.

"Bees are magnificent creatures. Without bees, the Earth that we know wouldn't exist."

"Without bees, Fort Womack wouldn't be on lockdown!" Shelby countered. "How about you get down off your soapbox and help us end this problem?"

Tom stood firm. "I won't help you destroy them."

Shelby turned and headed for the door. Derek rushed after her.

"Hold up," he said. "We need him."

"What for? It sounds like he's chosen a side, and it's not the human race."

"Shelby..."

"I'm an officer of the law, Derek. I swore to serve and protect."

"I know you did, but—"

Shelby whirled on him. "What if they came for Mel, hmm? What if they came for your daughter? I know what I'd do. I'd rip them apart with my bare hands if I had to."

That last bit was directed toward Tom, who looked as if he were ready with a rebuttal. Derek motioned for him to can it.

"Look, Shelby. Let's give the man a chance. If it's a bust, I'll take any flowers we harvest and hand them personally to Jim Mix."

Shelby's glare bored holes in him. "You're not planning on filming this little debacle, are you? With an eye toward selling the footage?"

"I hadn't thought about it—"

"Bullshit." She saw right through him.

"Fine. What would be the harm in that? You brought up Mel—would it be so terrible if I could sell some footage and keep a roof over that girl's head?"

Shelby looked from Derek to Tom. "You two are *perfect* for each other."

As she headed for the door, her phone blipped, stopping her in her tracks.

"Thanks for the assist, honey, but I'll be swinging Derek by as soon as..." She paused and listened intently. "What do you mean? Okay. We'll be right there." She waved to Derek. "Come on."

"What is it?" Derek asked, his skin prickling. "Is Mel all right?"

"I don't know," Shelby said. "Justine can't find her."

Mel and her fellow campers traipsed dutifully after Mr. Armbrister, loaded down with gear. Their regimented leader had insisted they deposit their devices in what he called his ditty bag, whatever that was, and now they were experiencing collective phone withdrawal.

"You can't truly see nature if your nose is in your phone," the man had said, scooping up their iPhones, Galaxies, and Pixels.

"But Mr. Armbrister..." Henry Swink moaned.

"But nothing, Mr. Swink," Mr. Armbrister barked. "I've been leading these trips for more than twenty years, and in that time, I watched my campers turn their attention more and more to their wretched screens and less to the scenic landscape. Not on my watch. Now, shall we proceed?"

The man led them on a curious journey through pasture-land and the first inklings of foothills, all the while ignoring posted notices that shouted *Private Property, Government Use Only,* and *Danger! Keep Out.*

When they reached the mouth of the canyon, not only was a cool breeze from within there to greet them but also an imposing metal gate that stretched across the gravel road leading deeper into the interior. A yellow metal sign announced: *Thunder Canyon – Closed to the Public.*

"Looks like we can't get in, Mr. A," Miguel Salida said with feigned sorrow. "Guess I better call my mom."

Mr. Armbrister lifted a lanyard from around his neck. Dangling from the end was a bronze key.

"I have friends in Parks and Wildlife," he said with a snicker.

He slipped the key into the padlock and it opened with a click. Mr. Armbrister quickly loosened the chain holding the gate shut and swung it open with a rusty whine.

"Bug collectors, welcome to Thunder Canyon!"

TWENTY-TWO

Mayor Guffey shielded her eyes from the sun as the deep *whump-whump* of the helicopter's rotors grew ever closer to Johnson Park. Mix's mode of transportation was unique—a retrofitted Firehawk with the Big Jim Mix logo emblazoned across the sides.

"That's an S-70," Chief Cross said, sauntering to the mayor's side.

"Looks like one of those copters that beat back the Pine Ridge Fire."

"Same animal," Cross said. "And they don't come cheap."

"Neither does Mr. Mix, I'd venture to guess," the mayor replied.

"You want this problem to go away? You're going to have to pay up."

"I'm sure we can move some funds out of the police budget."

"Over my dead body."

The helicopter slowly descended, touching down on the grassy green where *As You Like It* was originally meant to be in full swing. Mayor Guffey sighed. There was always next year, but would the crowds return after a blow like this? She could almost see her opponent's ads for the next election. *"Did you vote for Mayor Guffey? Stings, doesn't it?"*

"Screw it," she said. "I guess I'll be approving that new parking meter proposal."

Two men exited the helicopter, ducking low as they made their way out of range of the still-spinning blades. A crew of about eight followed behind. The mayor instantly recognized the man clutching the big Stetson hat as Jim Mix. *Big* Jim Mix, as he'd branded himself. She knew folks said "everything was bigger in Texas"—hell, it seemed like half of the Colorado population now consisted of Texans with their monster-sized dually trucks and belt buckles the size of pancakes—but Mix had taken the motto to heart. He was Falstaff in a cowboy hat.

The man trying to keep pace with Mix was slight in comparison. He wore a light linen suit and scampered like a rabbit. Mix's "bee expert" was in desperate need of a sandwich or two.

"Madam Mayor!" Mix drawled, arms outstretched. "Beautiful town, you got here. Shame what happened. But we're gonna set things right, ain't we, Mr. Gale?"

Despite working for a local university, Jefferson Gale huffed and puffed like a tourist from sea level. He dabbed at his forehead with a handkerchief.

"Thank you for dropping everything on such short notice, Mr. Mix," Mayor Guffey said, shaking the man's massive hand. "I'm eager to hear what you've got planned for us."

"That would be a rather short discussion, if you ask me,"

the man said. "Find the critters; kill the critters. Am I hitting close to the mark?"

"That's a bullseye, Mr. Mix."

"Before I started chasing storms," Mix said, "I tracked big game. First rule of game hunting is to tag the beast on the first shot; otherwise, the animal is gonna be taking *you* home as a trophy rather than the other way around."

"I'd say what we've got here is a hell of a lot different than tracking lions or tigers or bears," Chief Cross offered.

"Which is why this fellow here is gonna be indispensable, eh, Mr. Gale?" Mix clapped Gale on the back, starting him wheezing all over again.

"Have you...excuse me," Gale panted, getting right to business. "Have you procured a specimen for me?"

"We've done you one better," Cross said, motioning to a nearby officer.

The young officer walked to the chief's vehicle, popped the hatch, and retrieved a large cage—the type animal control used to relocate pesky raccoons. Inside, awake and angry as hell, were two of the disturbingly large bees.

"Meet Romeo and Juliet," Cross said, taking the cage from the officer and handing it over to Gale.

Jefferson Gale stared down at the bees almost lovingly, Mayor Guffey observed, even when they became agitated and tried to sting him through the wire mesh. And was he... humming to them?

"These are worker bees," Gale said. "Hence, they're both female. If you wish to stick with Shakespearean designations, might I suggest we address our apian friends as Beatrice and Hero?"

"I beg your pardon?" Cross asked.

"From *Taming of the Shrew,*" Mayor Guffey said, proud of herself.

"*Much Ado About Nothing,* actually," Gale replied. He walked over to an upended trash can and set the cage atop it. He then reached into his jacket, produced a zippered leather wallet, opened it, and extracted what looked like a long dental instrument with pincers at one end.

"We have a room at the municipal building where you can set up," the mayor said, but Gale waved her off.

"All in good time."

Mix leaned in and whispered in Mayor Guffey's ear. "The man's an eccentric, but he knows his stuff."

"Let's hope so," she replied.

Gale removed a small pillbox from his pocket and opened it. He carefully picked a small metal dot from the box with the instrument. Mayor Guffey thought the man looked like a watchmaker making fine adjustments to a timepiece.

"These are micro trackers," Gale said, gently placing the dot on one of the bees' backs. "The adhesive is quite strong. With the trackers in place, we should be able to monitor Beatrice and Hero's movements."

"And you think they'll just fly on back to their friends?" Cross scoffed. The mayor threw him a look, and he regulated his tone. "That's amazing."

"Yes, it is," Gale said as he applied the second dot on the other bee.

Trackers in place, the man reached for the cage's latch. Cross took a step forward, the mayor's withering looks be damned.

"I saw a man swell up like a sausage on a grill after just

one of those things lit into him. I think we'd better adjust our proximity."

He ushered Mix, the mayor, and Gale back to where a line of officers stood, audience to the proceedings. Cross then grabbed up a discarded stake, holding it out like a lance. With one deft move, he disarmed the latch. A panel dropped, exposing the bees to the outside world.

At first the insects were content to remain inside, but when Cross gave the cage a couple raps with the stake, the two bees leaped to life, buzzing and bouncing off the wire walls.

Jefferson Gale shocked everyone by dashing toward the cage, shooing the bees away.

"Fly! Be free!"

He's a nutcase, Mayor Guffey thought.

But the bees obeyed Gale, breaching the cage and taking wing.

"Parting is such sweet sorrow," Gale crooned as the bees disappeared into the summer sky.

TWENTY-THREE

As Shelby turned down the drive to the Odditorium, Derek spied Justine standing beside her Outback.

There was no sign of Mel.

Derek hopped out of the cruiser before Shelby had a chance to pull to a stop.

"Did you call her name?" he demanded. "Where did you look? Did you try her phone?"

Justine, having spent her life taming wild horses, spoke to Derek with the same soothing voice she'd used on countless angry stallions.

"Easy, Papa. If I can find a lone rattlesnake in a grazing pasture, I think I can find a little girl in her own house. She's not here. Besides—"

"Damn it, we should have come straight here," Derek cried.

"I was here fifteen minutes after Shelby called," Justine said. "Besides, like I was going to say—"

Derek ignored her and headed for the door.

"Mel?"

An oscillating fan ticked away, and the refrigerator hummed, but other than that, all was still.

Mel was nowhere to be seen.

Derek headed for the Odditorium section. Maybe his daughter had actually listened to him for once and was hiding away, safe and sound, beneath the Tommyknocker display. Maybe that's why Justine hadn't found her. Stranger things happened every day.

He quickstepped past the other displays until he came to the Tommyknocker's cave. He tossed aside one of the little mannequins and crawled into the fake cavern.

"Mel!"

The trapdoor was closed, but that didn't mean anything. Derek lifted the trap, hoping to be greeted by his daughter's shining face. Instead, all he found was the fog machine he'd bought at the Halloween Store gathering dust.

"Damn it."

He extracted himself from the cave to find Tom standing in the middle of the room, gazing around at the wide variety of exhibitions.

"Quite a setup you got here," Tom said, sounding sincerely impressed. "There's some stuff here we could use."

"Knock yourself out," Derek said, brushing past him.

Back in the living quarters, he found Shelby and Justine standing in front of the computer. Something was taped to the screen.

"Is that a note?" he asked.

"It is," Justine said. "And I would have told you about it if you'd given me half a chance."

Derek yanked the scrap of paper off the monitor. He and Mel always left messages for each other on the fridge door.

Leaving a note on the computer seemed to indicate that his daughter wanted him both to read it and *not* read it in equal measure.

> Dad,
> Don't worry. I am going camping with my nature club. Mr. Armbrister is driving. If something is important you do it. Sorry if you are mad.
> Mel

Derek balled up the note and threw it across the room. His face felt hot. He pulled his phone and quickly scrolled through his contact list. AAA Plumbers, Albertson Printing...

"What's this, Derek?" Shelby asked, sitting in front of the computer screen.

...Anderson Farms, Armbrister...

"Armbrister!" he cried aloud and hit dial.

The phone rang twice, then went to voicemail.

"This is Curt Armbrister. I can't take your call at the moment—"

"Damn it!"

He hung up and dialed again.

Meanwhile, Shelby stared intently at the monitor.

"This is Curt Armbrister. I can't take your call—"

Derek quickly practiced the message he was going to leave for Mr. Armbrister, editing out the expletives he wanted to hurl at the man for taking his child and worrying him half to death.

As he waited for the beep, he glanced down at the

computer screen in time to see Shelby hit play on an open video clip.

Molly appeared on screen, her hair whipping in the wind.

Derek froze.

"Turn that off."

Shelby ignored him. She was frozen in place as well.

"Come on, ten more minutes!" Molly laughed.

She stared directly into the camera—the camera attached to the helmet of the Tornado Suit.

"Shelby..." he implored.

Shelby sat transfixed, staring at her dead sister brought to life via video wizardry.

"Let's try again tomorrow," Derek heard himself say.

"The skies are perfect," Molly said. *"Where's Sir Derek the Bold when I need him?"*

"Heading back home before the storm hits!"

Molly took the helmet in both hands and spoke directly into the camera.

"What's our motto, huh? 'If it's important, we do it.'"

Derek tried to reach over Shelby's shoulder to shut off the video, but she rebuffed him. All he could do was watch the nightmare play itself out.

"Look!" Molly cried. *"The funnel is turning."*

The audio crackled.

"Molly, I don't think..."

The video garbled.

Maybe this time she gets away, Derek thought. Maybe this time...

The footage resumed. The sound of whipping wind blasted from the speakers. The screen was awash in swirling dust.

For a moment, the file glitched, and the picture froze: Derek, his arm outstretched; Molly, grabbing desperately for his hand.

And then she was gone, spinning upward, becoming nothing but a dot in the sky.

The video took pity on him and devolved into static, but the damage was done. Derek stumbled backward and dropped into the sofa.

"Think I'll wait outside," Justine said. She squeezed Shelby's shoulder and left Shelby and Derek the room.

Shelby swiveled in her chair to face Derek.

"I...don't know what to say."

"There's nothing to say."

Shelby wiped tears from her cheek. "You tried to get Molly to turn back. But she just had to be stubborn. She was always so stubborn."

Now it was Derek's turn to cry.

Shelby rose. For a second, Derek thought she meant to embrace him, but she held back.

"I always thought—"

"That I got her killed?"

"I'm sorry for that."

"I might as well have. It wasn't her idea to build the suit. None of this...not the suit, not the Odditorium...none of it was her idea."

Tom burst into the room, the fog machine in his arms.

"I'm taking this. Do you happen to have a generator on hand?"

Derek and Shelby turned in tandem, both avoiding his gaze.

"What did I miss?" Tom asked.

"I can't lose Mel too," Derek said. "I just can't."

"You know, it's almost as if you don't have a cop in the family." It was the first time Shelby had mentioned them being family since Molly's death.

Derek wiped his eyes. "What are you saying?"

"I'm saying you and Mr. Buckaroo go take care of the bee problem; Justine and I will track down Mel. Along with some of Fort Womack's finest, of course."

"Divide and conquer?"

"Divide and conquer."

Derek nodded. "I don't think the *Lightning Bug* can hold everything we need. Want to loan me the cruiser?"

"Very funny. You can take the Outback."

"You think Justine will be okay with that?"

"She'd better be," Shelby said, offering him a slight smile. "Otherwise, I'll slap the cuffs on her."

TWENTY-FOUR

Mayor Guffey wheeled herself into the municipal building's spare conference room where Mix and his people had set up. She only visited the building during crises—giving pep talks in the auditorium to folks displaced by wildfires or seeking out a warming station—and as such, the place gave her the creeps.

Jefferson Gale sat at a folding table in the middle of the room, hovering over a makeshift command center, complete with multiple laptops. The mayor was impressed. The new arrivals had jumped in feetfirst.

"Do you have a fix on them yet?" Mayor Guffey asked, announcing herself to the room.

"Just minutes away, isn't that right, Mr. Gale?" Mix replied.

Gale didn't answer, just kept tapping away at a keyboard.

"Just a few minutes," Mix said, answering for his colleague. "May I offer you some coffee?"

"Did we provide it?"

"Yes, you did, and thank you."

"I'll pass." She paused. Now was as good a time as any. "So, Mr. Mix, about your fee..."

The Texan waved her off. "Let's have a chinwag about that down the road a stretch, shall we?"

"I need to have a ballpark figure if you don't mind. There are boards and committees I have to answer to."

"Look," Mix said, laying on the charm. "We both know that when I pull this off, all those nature channels are gonna be knocking down my door for footage, interviews, merchandise, you name it."

"Great," the mayor said. "So you're going to do this for us gratis?"

"Wish I could, Madam Mayor, wish I could. But I just pooled all my resources so I could help you good folks out." He smiled broadly. "And that weren't cheap, believe you me."

"Which brings me back to my point, Mr. Mix—"

"I've got one!" Gale cried.

Excited, Mix grabbed hold of the mayor's chair and pushed her over to where Gale sat, staring at a screen. "See? What did I say? We're on this."

Touch my chair one more time, and I'll break your kneecaps, Mayor Guffey thought. But what she said was, "That's great news. Where is it?"

Gale tapped at a digital topo map on the screen. "That would be roughly three miles northwest of town. Out by your reservoir."

"And the second bee?"

Gale didn't answer right away. "Uh...about half a mile north of that."

"Can you pull up their paths from where we released them to where they are now?" Mix asked Gale.

"Of course I can."

With a few clicks of his mouse, Gale brought up an overlay of the current screen. Two meandering red lines, both starting at the same point, veered off in wildly different directions. If they were supposed to return to the swarm, it sure looked like it was news to them.

The mayor shifted in her chair. "It looks like Beatrice and Hero are off sightseeing. How lovely for them."

"I don't understand," Gale puzzled. "Maybe they were injured somehow and can't locate the colony. Maybe—"

"Maybe I should start looking at some alternatives," the mayor grumbled.

"Madam Mayor…" Mix protested.

"Hold on!" Gale's foot started tapping a mile a minute. The man truly was half-rabbit. "Look."

Mayor Guffey looked, and a smile spread across her face.

The two lines were bending toward each other. The bees were converging. The trio watched as the twin flight paths merged into one.

"They've picked up the scent!" Mix crowed, slapping Gale on the back. "Let's go, folks. The clock is ticking."

"Mr. Mix? Mr. Mix!" the mayor said. "What's happening?"

Big Jim Mix waved his Stetson over his head. "Why, we're going bee hunting. That's what's happening!"

TWENTY-FIVE

"This feels wrong," Derek said, turning off the main highway onto the county road leading to the crevasse. "I should have gone with her."

"With your sis, the cop?"

"Yeah."

"I disagree. I need you here. How about we stay focused and stick to the plan."

"What if—"

"You'll drive yourself crazy what-iffing like that. Think about it this way, Stratton," Tom said, adjusting the Outback's AC. "If we draw the swarm to us, your daughter—no matter *where* she is—will be where they *ain't.*"

"Do you have kids, Tom?"

"Not to my knowledge."

"Then excuse me if I say that doesn't help one bit."

Tom sighed. "Roger that."

The sun wasn't down, wouldn't be for a couple of hours, but the sky had taken on an orangish hue. Shelby had called Molly stubborn, and his wife was certainly that. And it was becoming all too clear that she had passed that particular trait on to their only daughter. They would have a long talk, he and his child, but right now all he wanted was a call from Shelby saying Mel was okay, and she was taking her to McDonald's for a post-search meal. His phone remained stubbornly silent. He checked for texts. Zip.

"If it makes you feel any better, I once lost my sister's kid at Casa Bonita. You know, that big ol' restaurant with the indoor cliff divers? More like a theme park than an actual restaurant, if you ask me—"

"Tom."

"Yeah, yeah, I know. Not helping."

The foothills stood watch over whatever trouble the two fools in the borrowed Subaru were about to get into. Derek knew Tom was right. If their scheme worked, and they managed to seal off the bees below ground, not only would they be hailed as heroes—with all the benefits that might bring, such as a forgiven eviction—but they'd be keeping *all* of Fort Womack's children safe, not just his.

"Here we are," Derek said as he pulled up to the crevasse.

He and Tom got out of the car and quickly set about unpacking the equipment. The sky was growing red—it was shaping up to be a beautiful Colorado evening. At least they wouldn't be trying to lure thousands of prehistoric bees their way in a thunderstorm. The bees were bad enough.

"All right," Tom said. "Let's get cracking."

Derek gassed up the portable Honda generator he'd bought for taking Mel and Molly camping. But getting the Odditorium up and running proved to be more of a time-stealer than he'd expected, and the three of them never actually made it up into the mountains. Sure, they'd taken in the occasional day hike, but their tent remained tucked away with their unused cross-country skis and kayak.

Now, Mel was out there somewhere camping without him.

"Next time, we go together," he said, unaware he'd spoken aloud.

"Sure, whatever you say," Tom replied, staring quizzically at him.

The first part of the plan was simple. Tom was a whiz at maneuvering the drone. The only concern was whether or not the signal would be strong enough once it flew down the great hole. Once below, he'd seek out the flowers, pick them with the drone's arm, and return to the surface. The next part entailed pulverizing the plants and mixing them in a water/alcohol solution to be fed into the fog machine from the Tommyknocker display. All that was left to do was hook the fog machine to the generator, fire it up, and hope the resultant psychedelic cloud would draw the bees like moths to a flame.

"Let's get this party started," Tom said.

The Bogie 99-G hovered momentarily over the crevasse as Tom tested its many features. Lights? Check. Camera? Check. Retractable arm? Check and double-check.

"Here goes nothing," Tom whispered, gritting his teeth.

The drone descended, buzzing like an oversized gnat.

"How's it holding up?" Derek asked, staring over Tom's shoulder at the miniature screen on the remote.

"So far, so good. If you're a praying man, I'd say get to it."

Tom switched to night vision, and the inner workings of the cavern lit up on the screen in garish white and green. The video coming back to the surface reminded Derek of that taken by deep-sea submersibles. The only thing missing was a circling shark.

"There!" Tom let out a whoop.

The man didn't have to explain—Derek could see the flowers clearly enough, albeit through an emerald filter.

"How's that for service?" Tom asked.

"Great. You think that arm is going to work?"

"Oh, ye of little faith!"

Tom worked the controls, and the arm lowered. With a couple of deft moves of his fingers, he latched the grabbing hand around a clump of flowers that appeared to have already been cut. Which one of the kids had precut the plants for them? And where were they now? One was in the hospital, but there hadn't been just one, had there?

"Aaa-aand, up we go."

Tom took it slowly. A couple of flowers slipped out of the drone's grip, but when the Bogie 99-G emerged from the fissure, it still had a floral bounty in its hand.

Derek stepped forward, eager to relinquish the drone of its load, but Tom stopped him.

"Grab some gloves, man! These things are already giving me a contact high."

Derek did as he was told, and soon the first harvest lay at the bottom of a plastic storage bin.

The drone made three more successful trips, each time returning to the surface with a phosphorescent bouquet. On its next journey to the center of the earth, Tom encountered a snag.

"Damn it."

"What's the problem?" Derek asked, catching himself before scratching an itch with a pollen-coated glove.

"That's all the loose stuff. The drone doesn't seem to have enough oomph to pull the rest free."

To illustrate, he held out the remote and let Derek take a peek at the screen. Sure enough, the drone's arm was extended, its hand gripping a large sunflower-like plant. Tom gave the flying vehicle the order to rise, but the flower it held had different plans.

"Do you think we have enough already?" Derek asked, scanning the plants in the bin. Tom needn't answer—Derek knew they needed more. Much more.

"I think it's coming..." Tom said.

He gave the drone an extra boost from the joystick, and it tilted dangerously to the side. The screen showed nothing but rock wall.

"Shit, shit, shit!" Tom shouted.

He eased off the controls, but it was no use. The drone corrected too much in the opposite direction and slammed against the cavern wall. It tumbled out of control, the video feed flickering as it struck, and landed on its side, teetering on the edge of a rock shelf.

"I guess it's time to pull out Plan B," Tom said.

"What's Plan B?"

"One of us has to go down there."

Derek shook his head. "Not a chance."

Tom pointed at the flower bin. "That's not nearly enough to pique their interest."

"Well, it's going to have to do."

"If the Pizza Hut buffet consisted of only breadsticks, would you even bother?"

"What are you even talking about?"

"We've got one shot at this, Stratton. One. We need to go down there—"

"You mean *I* need to go down there."

"Fine. You need to go down, rip up as much as you can, and get your ass back up so we can have a chance at…at…"

Tom froze.

"Tom?" Derek snapped his fingers. "Tom!"

"I…"

Already frustrated with the man, Derek stormed over to where Tom stood staring down at the remote and swiped the device out of his hands.

"What's got you so spooked?"

Derek glanced down at the little screen, and his throat clenched. There, glowing green thanks to the night vision setting, was a young man's swollen face, his eyes staring blankly ahead.

TWENTY-SIX

Tom grabbed the remote from Derek's hands and fell to his knees. He bashed it against a rock, over and over again, until it broke apart, and his hands were bleeding.

Derek pulled him to his feet.

"Easy, Tom." He felt like Justine taming one of her horses. "Breathe."

"I sent that boy to his death!"

"No, you did not."

Tom ran his hands through his hair. The man was losing it. "If I hadn't pointed him your way—"

"Yeah," Derek said firmly, "and if I hadn't given him the map. Someone once told me a person can drive themself crazy what-iffing like that."

"The boy is dead! Killed by those...those..."

"All the more reason to get this over with so it doesn't happen to anyone else."

Tom seized the front of Derek's shirt. "If this doesn't work, Stratton..."

"Yes?"

"We have to exterminate them. Every last buzzing one of them."

Derek cocked his head. "What happened to 'bees are magnificent creatures'?"

"If it comes to it, I'll blast them out of the sky myself."

Derek removed Tom's hands from his shirt.

"Let's make sure it doesn't come to that."

Derek headed for the pile of equipment and began rooting through it, coming up with a length of rope and a coil of bungee cord. He then proceeded to tie the rope and bungee together—muscle memory giving new life to a childhood obsession with knots—and attached the line to the Outback's trailer hitch.

"What do you think you're doing?" Tom said, still shaken.

"How far down do you think the drone went?"

"Uh...twenty? Thirty feet?"

Derek made a mental calculation. With both the rope and the bungee, he might have enough line to reach the same depth the drone had. *Might.*

The only flashlight he'd been able to find on such short notice was of the squeeze variety—no battery required but plenty of lever-squeezing in order to keep it lit.

He tossed Tom the keys to the Subaru.

"Thank you, Derek."

"What for?"

"For not making me go down there." Tom looked like he was about to lose it all over again.

"No problem, Tom."

Derek didn't have any climbing gear, and as such, an old

backpack served as a makeshift harness. He feared his armpits were going to be raw by the end of his efforts as the arm straps took the brunt of his weight, but the pack was Army surplus, made out of material built to survive World War III. If there was a weak link in the plan, it wouldn't be the backpack or the rope or the car to which it was attached—it would be the man with zero spelunking skills whatsoever.

"Once I'm down, keep a careful watch on the line," Derek instructed. "When I'm ready to come up, I'll give the rope a 'shave and a haircut.'"

"Huh?"

Derek demonstrated the beat by clapping. *Clap clap-clap-clap clap, clap clap.*

"Roger that," Tom replied.

Derek had hoped that Tom could lower him down by hand to avoid the rope fraying against the rock lip of the crevasse, but he had a good fifty pounds on ol' Buckaroo, and he had no interest in accidentally dragging Tom down into the earth with him. They'd have to risk letting the car ease him down, rope friction or no rope friction.

As soon as Tom had driven the car a few yards away and the line was taut, Derek gave him the thumbs-up. He looked skyward.

"Molly, if you're listening, I could use all the help I can get. Put in a good word, will ya?"

With that, he eased himself over the edge.

Derek had known the backpack would cut into his flesh, but he wasn't prepared for the intensity of the pinch. He was afraid both of his arms would go numb and wriggled them about to relieve his screaming nerves. He achieved a modicum of success, settling for a dull aching pressure instead.

The lower he dropped, the darker it got, and he suddenly realized he hadn't been pumping his flashlight. A few squeezes later, the cavern lit up an unnatural blue-white.

He could smell the flowers already, and their scent alone was making him light-headed. He tried to calculate how far he'd come but figured it didn't really matter. Once he reached the end of the rope, that was the end of the ride.

Waving the flashlight about, Derek caught sight of something in the beam. A few more feet, and he could see the thing clearly: it was the upended drone.

He girded himself. If he was low enough to see the drone, he was low enough to see the college kid's lifeless body.

While he was positioning himself to land on the rock shelf beside the crashed drone, the line momentarily went slack. Derek dropped a good two feet before the rope went taut, but those two feet might as well have been two hundred the way his stomach reacted.

"Easy up there!" he called, even though there was no way Tom would hear his protestation.

Derek's feet touched solid rock, and he quickly shined the flashlight about, spotting a cluster of multicolored flowers directly below him.

He also found the young caver.

The kid was still wearing his climbing harness, despite the fact that his body had swollen so much that it had ripped the seams of his clothing. A frayed length of caving line lay at his feet. He had a massive head of hair, and his eyes peered out from under his bangs, blank and unseeing. The lower half of his face was bloated and purple—he'd taken a sting directly to the chin.

Derek pulled a stash of zip ties from his back pocket and grabbed the nearest patch of flowers, giving them a tug. The plants held firm.

Damn.

Derek had brought a number of things with him down the hole, but a knife was not one of them. Had he really gotten this close only to be thwarted for lack of a knife?

He checked the blades of the inoperative drone and found them to be too thin and flexible to cut anything. He considered bashing the drone apart, as Tom had the remote, and using its shattered pieces to hack away at the plants, but something in the kid's hand caught his eye.

Despite his aversion to doing so, Derek leaned in close, nervously squeezing away at the flashlight to give him the best lighting possible.

In the kid's swollen hand was a Leatherman tool.

"Thanks, Molly," Derek whispered, reaching for the implement. He gently but firmly pulled the tool out of the kid's grasp.

The "dead" body lying in front of him gasped.

The kid's alive!

The young man with the shaggy mane reached for him blindly. He tried to speak, but with his tongue protruding from his mouth, he only managed an unnerving raspberry.

Derek scooted around the rock shelf, mindful of the drop-off, and placed a hand on the kid's shoulder.

"Don't worry. You're going to be okay," he lied.

The kid mumbled in response. He sucked air, and the sound was like someone slurping up the last mouthful of a milkshake. It was amazing that he was alive, but the miracle would be short-lived unless Derek could somehow get him topside.

Derek took the briefest of pauses, then launched his new plan. Using the Leatherman, he freed as many flowers as he could. He removed the backpack/harness and stuffed the flowers inside. He repeated this until the pack was almost overflowing. Then, he worked the kid's arms into the pack's straps, and cinched the strap across his chest. He had to adjust the straps' length due to the guy's engorged arms, but he somehow pulled it off.

Derek lifted the kid's chin.

"We're getting you out of here."

He tugged on the rope, counting out the signal for Tom to hoist away. He waited for Tom to get the message, get back in the car, and begin pulling him—or the kid, rather—back up the throat of the crevasse.

He waited. And nothing happened.

"Come on, Buckaroo," he whispered.

The kid burbled in response.

"Save your breath," Derek said, before yanking on the rope a second time.

Still nothing.

Despite feeling like the operation had been going well so far, Derek got the distinct impression it was about to go south. He never knew when good luck was coming his way, but *bad* luck? He could smell it coming a mile away.

"Tom!" he shouted upward. His voice ricocheted off the rock walls, no doubt losing all steam before making it to the surface. What was going on up there?

He tugged again, and this time, the line jerked. It did so

with such urgency it lifted the college kid off his feet, dangling him in midair like the world's largest marionette.

For a moment, all was still, save for the young man's pained wheezing. Then, the guy shot upward, disappearing into the darkness above.

Derek was alone, some thirty feet below the surface, with no way of getting back up.

That's when he heard it.

At first, he thought it might just be wind blowing across the opening of the fissure, turning the entire crevasse into a natural musical instrument.

But as the sound came into focus, Derek knew that he was dead wrong. It wasn't the wind he heard but the mounting buzz of approaching bees.

TWENTY-SEVEN

The old familiar fear rose up like a viper threatening to bite, and Derek fought it back. *They're coming! Jump for it. Better to die on the rocks below!*

"Enough!" Derek bellowed, drowning out the wailing voice in his head. He didn't have time for childhood anxieties —he had to get out of there, pronto.

Could he climb up? He tested the idea and failed miserably. Only a professional free solo climber could best the fissure.

Could he grab Tom's attention? Pointing the feeble flashlight upward only made him laugh. The beam made it about ten feet before petering out.

"You're running out of options," he said, prodding himself. *Think, man, think.*

The sound overhead grew ever louder, and he couldn't help but imagine the scene topside: Tom struggling to get the injured kid into the car, the swarm descending, bees attacking left and right while the setting sun painted the horrific scene red. Derek thought he heard a scream, or was it his own? He was losing his grip. The stillness below and the chaos above made war with each other, threatening to drive him mad.

Derek felt like he was about to crack when something hit him in the head. The blow was sudden and shocking and almost toppled him over into darkness below. No need for flowers at his funeral—he'd spend eternity among them.

He reached up, grabbing for whatever had struck him and found it to be the makeshift backpack harness. And lo and behold, the rope line was still attached.

Good old Tom!

He wasted no time reeling in the backpack and readjusting the straps to fit his less ample arms. But just as he was about to don the pack, the slack rope went taut, and he instinctually tightened his grip. Before he had a second to think, he was rapidly ascending, holding on singlehandedly.

Derek dropped the flashlight as he rushed upward. The muscles in his forearm screamed and his fingers threatened to cramp. There was nothing to do but hold on, and hold on he did, though his arm felt like it was being ripped out of its socket.

He was concentrating so hard on maintaining his grip that he was taken completely off guard when he plowed into a sharp stone that jutted from the wall's side. Not that he could have prepared for it. But the rock's edge sliced a gash in his bicep, making holding on exponentially more difficult.

The surface was fast approaching. The rope only had to hold for a few more feet...

And then he was out of the hole and racing across the ground, dragged by the Outback.

Relief flooded over him, and he quickly let go of the pack.

Unfortunately, that didn't stop his forward movement. Perplexed, he strained to see what the holdup was. In his hasty climb to the surface, his hand had become hopelessly tangled in one of the pack's straps. Being pulled up a rock crevasse was no picnic; being dragged across the plains was no better.

"Stop!" he cried fruitlessly. Tom had his foot down hard on the gas and was not relenting. Derek slammed against rocks, weeds, more rocks. If this lasted much longer, the ground rushing beneath him would power-sand the skin right off him.

Derek thought quickly. What had he done with the Leatherman? He whispered a silent prayer that he'd put it back in his pocket and praised heaven when his free fingers located it. He flicked open the blade and reached above his head. As he sawed at the strap, he saw the swarm swirling above, blotting out the last rays of sunlight.

He was just about through the fabric when his forward progress suddenly stopped. Derek heard frantic footfalls, and then, Tom was pulling him up to sitting.

"I thought I lost you back there!" Tom cried.

"Where's the kid?" Derek asked, pulling himself free of the strap. The pack itself was empty. Good. Hopefully Tom had put his harvest somewhere safe, although "safe" was not a word one used with swarming bees circling overhead.

"In the back seat. He's not doing so good. Oh my God! Your arm—"

"It's fine. We can't stay out here in the open."

"But, our plan—"

"No time!" Derek yelled, struggling to his feet.

No time was right—the swarm was shifting its configu-

166

ration, bees at the center dropping lower, drawing down the rest. The buzzing tornado was forming, and when complete, it would take out anything in its path.

"We've got to run. Where the hell did they come from? And why are they here?"

Tom's eyes looked past him. Derek followed his gaze.

Heading their way, traveling low and fast, was a helicopter. Not some small puddle-jumper but one of those massive beasts that firefighters flew into the blaze.

Mix.

Tom helped Derek to the Outback and set him in the passenger seat. The kid from the cavern moaned in the back seat, the smell of recent regurgitation heavy in the car.

"Be right back," Tom said.

Derek grabbed his arm. "What the hell?"

"I got us into this mess, and I'll get us out of it."

"What are you talking about?"

"CO_2! Exploding dynamite gives off CO_2!" Tom shouted, slamming the door. "One stick down the hole should draw them in. And when it does...*blammo!*" With that, he raced off toward the crevasse.

"You idiot!" Derek fumed. The kid in the back moaned even louder. "Not you."

He twisted about in his seat and stared out the back window. The damn fool was heading toward the pile of equipment they'd unloaded. He was going for the dynamite.

The bee tornado touched ground. Dust flew. The stage was set: Tom racing for the dynamite, bees pouring out of the sky. And into the mix came Mix in his copter. There were three pieces on the board, each liable to take out the other two.

No, not three pieces. *Four.* The Subaru, with two injured passengers and no driver, was a pawn if ever there was one. But Derek had learned early in life that pawns could sometimes win the game.

He worked his way over the middle armrest and into the driver's seat, his body screaming at him and calling him every name in the book. Once behind the wheel, he threw the car into drive.

"Hold on, kid," he instructed.

First step? Head Tom off at the pass. Get him back into the car and *away* from the swarm. Next? He would deal with "next" when he got there.

Steering his way toward the crazy old man, Derek spied the helicopter in his rearview mirror. *Objects in mirror are closer than they appear.* Whatever Mix had in mind, Derek wanted to be well clear before the copter reached ground zero.

A second later, he caught up with Tom, the man's frizzy hair made even more frizzy by his dash for the dynamite. Derek rolled down the passenger side window.

"Get in!"

Tom either didn't hear or didn't listen—he kept on running.

"Get in *now*, you sonofabitch!"

Still, no response.

Determined to pluck the man out of harm's way, he momentarily put Tom *in* harm's way by speeding up and veering sharply to the right, blocking the running man's path. Tom, for his part, didn't slow. Instead, he barreled headlong into the side of the Subaru.

"Agh!" Tom shouted.

Derek reached over and tugged on the door handle. "I'm not telling you again," he shouted in his best "dad" voice. "Get...in!"

A lone bee made a dive for the car. It moved at such velocity that when it headbutted Tom, it knocked him off his feet.

"Tom!"

Derek strained to look out the passenger door, trying desperately to locate the downed Buckaroo. But the bee must have sensed him—or *smelled* him—and chittered angrily. It advanced, and as it did, Derek slammed the door shut, pinning the giant insect half in and half out of the car. He tugged on the door until he heard the bee's exoskeleton *crunch*. Its antennae went limp, creamy ooze dripping from its lifeless mandibles.

Derek looked up. Tom was back on the run. He reached the red storage locker and extracted a stick of the explosive. Didn't the man know it was suicide run? Did he even care?

When Derek later described what happened, he struggled to keep the order of events straight, so rapidly did they tumble, one to the next.

He saw Tom light the dynamite and hold it aloft. But before the man had a chance to toss it, Mix's helicopter swooped past, releasing a thick cloud of mist from its underbelly.

Disoriented, the swarm broke in all different directions, like a panicked crowd dispersing. Some of the bees banked right toward the hills; others took off across the grasslands to the left. A few, to Derek's dismay, seemed to decide that Tom was to blame, and they attacked.

Half a dozen bees lit into Tom, stinging him in rapid succession, knocking the dynamite to the ground.

Shit. He's blown himself up.

Tom scrambled to pick up the dynamite, its fuse almost spent. He raised the stick high above his head, readying his throw. "Get out of here!"

Derek threw the Subaru into drive and hit the gas. Bees buffeted the car, sounding like a vicious hailstorm. Derek spun the wheel and set off toward the plains, hoping to put as much distance between himself and the explosive before it...

The shockwave cause by the detonating dynamite struck the rear window, pelting Derek with beads of glass. A cluster of fallen fence posts loomed up ahead. Derek tried to steer clear, but it was too late.

He plowed into the posts, and everything went black.

TWENTY-EIGHT

M el lay in her solo tent, listening to a group of boys giggling in theirs. She would have checked the time, but her phone was still on lockdown in Mr. Armbrister's ditty bag.

The evening had consisted of bug trapping, bug identifying, and bug lectures by Mr. A. During the trek to the interior of Thunder Canyon, she'd wondered why she was sneaking behind her father's back. Maybe it was the way he wouldn't listen to her. Maybe it was the video she'd found on the hard drive, the one that ended with her mother screaming. Maybe it was all those things and more. Life had never gotten back on track since they'd lost Mom, and Mel found herself eager to lash out in all sorts of ways. Like sneaking out on a bug hunt.

Mr. A's lectures had actually turned out to be fascinating, and the stories he told about previous camping trips had the whole group in stitches, especially the tale of the golf ball-sized hail and the flimsy tent. Bobby Lamar had almost wet himself laughing.

Mel decided that the *real* reason she'd snuck out was because she found it hard looking at Dad. Ever since Mom died, he was either trying too hard or too little, and she never knew which face he'd be wearing from one day to the next.

Better to play hooky and take to the hills. She knew she'd pay for it later, but consequences had never been her primary concern.

"Who farted?" one of the boys cried, and the rest burst out laughing, offering up their best imitations of gas passing for approval. *Boys.*

"Get some sleep," an exhausted Mr. A called from his tent. The boys did quiet down, but their flatulent comedy routines continued in hushed tones.

Mel suddenly felt a strong urge to go home. It started as a tickle in her gut and built to a full-body ache. What made it all the worse was she knew it wasn't home she was lonely for —it was Mom. They'd never gone camping together, and now they never would. It was a different kind of pain than stubbing your toe or skinning your knee; it didn't live in just one part of the body but the whole thing.

Pp-pp-ffft!

The boys were at it again. Mel rolled over in her sleeping bag, the lumpy ground doing its best to ensure she awakened sore and unrested. With the boys' antics playing soundtrack, she closed her eyes and willed herself to sleep. As she let go of the day, she pictured her mother in her mind's eye. And she was laughing.

"Love you, Mom," Mel whispered to the night.

TWENTY-NINE

"I love you, Molly," Derek sighed.

He opened his eyes and was surprised to find himself not in his bed at home with his wife by his side, but on an army cot in an empty office. He sat up quickly and instantly regretted it. His head felt like it had been bashed apart and put back together again by a chimp. He'd always thought seeing double was the stuff of cartoons, but when he looked down at his feet, he saw four of them.

"Hello?"

As he stretched his arms, the pain that shot through his bicep acted like a sudden slap, jolting him awake from his slumber. He looked down at his arm. A dressing had been applied to his wound—a line of blood darkened the gauze.

"Is anybody here?"

A harried EMS worker appeared at the door. "Good, you're up. How are we doing? How's the arm? How's the head?"

Derek wanted to reply that the head felt like crap and the

arm even worse, but instead, he simply said, "I'm okay. Where's Tom and the kid? Are they okay?"

"I don't know who you're talking about, sir. Things are kind of crazy right now, as you'd imagine. We're all pulling double duty, Mister...?"

"Stratton," Derek offered. "I think. What time is it?"

He rose, and the EMS worker motioned him to sit back down. "You need to rest."

"What time is it?" Derek asked louder.

"Five-thirty."

"In the morning?" Derek asked, fighting the urge to puke. The double vision was back and playing havoc with his sense of balance. Had he really been out that long? "Where am I?"

"Municipal building. One of the admin offices." She motioned again for him to sit. "Sir, if you would."

He ignored her and headed for the door.

"No problem," the EMS worker said, throwing up her hands. "The mayor said to keep an eye on you, but if you're determined to be a dick, go be a dick somewhere else. We need the bed."

"The mayor?" Derek asked. "Where is she?"

He found Mayor Guffey and Chief Cross huddled over a table in an upstairs conference room. They were listening intently to a slight man seated at what he could only imagine was some sort of command center—laptops, screens, shortwave radios.

Jim Mix was there too, and when he saw Derek swaying

in the doorway, he extricated himself from the ongoing conversation.

"Jesus, Stratton, you look like a dog's breakfast. Good to see you upright."

"What the hell happened, Mix? Where's Tom Buckaroo? Where's..." Derek winced as a stab of pain ran up his arm.

"Come on," the Texan said, taking Derek by his good arm and leading him out of the room.

Mix ushered Derek into a storage room filled with reams of paper and a humming copy machine, and closed the door. "Things are a little tense in there. Figured we could use a little privacy, you and I."

"Where's Tom?"

Mix sucked on his teeth. "ICU or the morgue, one or the other."

"And the kid?"

"Same. They were in bad shape, both of them. Nothing we can do about that right now. They're in God's hands. What I've got in *my* hands is this mess you left me with."

"How so?" As woozy as Derek felt, he was still picking up on the aggression coming off Mix.

"The mayor sent me to do a job. I was doing the job, and then...whoopsie-daisy! There you were, you and that old beekeeper friend of yours, smack dab in the middle of my business. What the ever-loving hell were you two doing out there?"

Derek hesitated. Could he trust Mix? The man had an ego bigger than the state from which he hailed, but he also had resources. And the mayor's ear.

"We were gathering flowers."

Mix didn't even crack a grin. "How quaint."

"To lure the bees."

The Texan sighed heavily and shook his head. "I always took you for a pragmatist, Stratton. Eccentric, sure—who in this business ain't. But forgive me if I say that as 'experts,' you and Buckaroo are sounding more and more like you're all hat and no cattle."

Derek brought his fist down on the copier, which proceeded to spit out blank sheets of paper. "Just listen, will you?"

"I'm all ears."

"The flowers are psychoactive. That means—"

"I know what that means, son."

"It's what they've been feeding on underground for eons. And now that they've been ripped out of the earth, they're going through some heavy-duty withdrawal. Those flowers are like heroin to a junkie."

"Or blood to a shark," Mix mused.

"Exactly."

Mix leaned over and shut off the copier. It spun down with a sigh. "Was your flower picking successful?"

"It was. I think I managed to gather up enough before the bees hit. And before *you* came barreling onto the scene."

"If I hadn't, you, sir, would be nothing but a pincushion."

Derek paused for a breath. His head was spinning again. This conversation wasn't going the way he'd hoped it would.

"Let's team up. My bait; your fishing pole."

"Meaning?"

"Use the flowers I harvested, aerosolize them, and crop dust those buzzing bastards. Do that, and you can lure them wherever you want."

"Such as?"

Derek thought for a moment. "Thunder Canyon. It's been off-limits for years due to rockslides. Completely unpopulated. It would make the perfect trap. We could lure them there, box them in, and—"

"Oh, this is gonna be fun," Mix said with a sly grin. "Tell me, where might this stash of flowers be at present?"

Derek threw up his hands. "How should I know? I don't even know how I got here."

"Chief Cross took all of your equipment for safekeeping," Mix said, more to himself than to Derek. "I suppose he'd be the one to ask."

Derek leaned in. "You can take all the credit you want. I don't care."

"That's awful big of you, Stratton," Mix said, squeezing his shoulder. "Let's go see the chief, shall we?"

The two made for the conference room, and as they walked through the door, Mix spoke low in his ear.

"Sorry about this, Stratton. Nothing personal, but a roundup can only have one wrangler." Mix clapped his hands together to draw the group's attention. "Friends, the depth of this man's recklessness is beyond measure. Chief Cross, I suggest you take him into custody and let me do what I can before any more innocents are endangered."

"What the hell?" It was all Derek could manage.

Mix whirled on him so dramatically, he could have played the ShakesBeer Festival's main stage. "I pray the Lord watch over those poor souls you put in harm's way."

Cross nodded to one of his men, and before Derek knew what was happening, the officer turned him about, cuffed him, and marched him out of the room.

The last thing he heard coming from the conference room before the officer whisked him down a stairwell was Mix taking charge of the situation.

"Chief, let's talk about Mr. Stratton's flowers."

THIRTY

The wail of sirens had diminished, but not enough for Mayor Guffey to let down her guard. The bee attack had happened on her watch and in the middle of her baby, the ShakesBeer Festival. It was meant to be the jewel in the crown of her term as mayor. Now, she knew, her name would forever be associated with screaming citizens and bees gone berserk. She could already see the headlines: *Fans Flee Bee-Deviled Festival, Mayor's Malfeasance Magnifies Mayhem,* and *Guffey Fails to Foil Furious Flying Freaks.*

But not if she nipped this in the bud.

She stared across the park at Mix and his people, readying for their assault. Gale bopped about frenetically, checking equipment and barking orders. It was a big day for the little man, and he looked like he was enjoying every minute of it. Mix, on the other hand, had the stern look of a killer about him. A hunter. Good. She needed someone with ice in their veins running the show.

"You know, if they screw the pooch, this town is going to

blame you," Chief Cross said, startling her. How long had he been standing there?

"And if they succeed, they're the heroes, not me."

"It's a conundrum."

Mayor Guffey gritted her teeth. "It doesn't have to be."

"You're not suggesting what I think you're suggesting, are you?"

The mayor shrugged. "Couldn't hurt to have a few photos of me leading the charge, could it?"

"You've never been on a helicopter in your life!"

"So?"

"It's a miserable way to travel. Every time I go up in one of those contraptions, I puke my guts out."

"Thanks for the info."

"Don't mention it."

The mayor stared across the field. The team was boarding the helicopter. The whine of its motor told her that if she wanted to seize the bull by the horns, she'd better do it quickly.

"Wheel me over there."

Her order shocked Cross. "Last time I touched that chair of yours, you near about bit my head off."

"I think we both know my sprinting days are long gone. So, if you don't mind?"

Cross didn't argue. He simply said, "Yes, Madam Mayor," grabbed hold of her wheelchair, and swiftly steered her across the grassy field.

The copter's blades were rotating rapidly as they approached. Mix was at the door, preparing to close up, when he spied the chief and the mayor sprinting/rolling his way. He raised a single hand as if to say, *What gives?* Mayor

Guffey pointed at herself, then up. It was a rudimentary bit of conversation, but the two understood each other. Mix nodded and waved her aboard.

"Need help getting in?" Cross shouted over the din of the helicopter.

"Hardy har har," the mayor shouted back.

It took a couple of Mix's men as well as the chief to get her and her chair aboard, but they managed. Before Mix slid the door shut, Cross reached up and kissed Mayor Guffey's hand.

"You come home safe, you hear, hon?"

"Will do, sweetheart."

With that, Mix closed and locked the door. The helicopter ascended like a great beast ready to do battle, leaving Cross standing alone in the middle of the field, a cloud of dust slowly swallowing him whole.

THIRTY-ONE

"I'm such an idiot."

Derek's words echoed about the holding cell. The cinderblock walls couldn't care less—they'd heard it all.

He'd never felt so alone. When Molly was alive, the two of them had engaged in constant banter, bouncing ideas off each other, cracking jokes or offering subtle criticisms. The stuff that a marriage is built on.

"Maybe that's why I'm always talking to myself," he mused.

Maybe.

Derek shifted on the uncomfortable metal bench. "How do I do it, honey? How the hell do I go on without you?"

You just keep moving.

"That's easy for you to say."

I'm not saying it. You are.

"That's kind of the point I'm making."

Molly sighed inside his head. Her sighs were long and dramatic and sounded like air escaping a balloon.

Can we talk about something other than me for moment?

"Such as?"

Your daughter?

Derek noticed the glitch in the conversation. The give-away. His wife would have said *our* daughter, but he decided to let it pass and see what imagined Molly had to say.

"Shelby and Justine are out looking for her."

That's good. But what are you doing about finding her?

"What can I do about it? Not sure if you can see, hon, but I'm kind of incarcerated at the moment."

The man I married wouldn't let something like that stop him.

Now, that *did* sound like Molly. And the implication stung.

"You think I've taken my eye off the ball where Mel is concerned?"

Her silence spoke volumes.

"What, so I should just let a swarm of prehistoric bees ravage the town and not raise a hand to help?"

That's not what I'm saying—

"What *are* you saying?"

Silence again. Derek thought he had scared her off, that he'd broken the spell that allowed them to converse. But then, Molly's voice was back, clearer than ever.

You know how you won me over, don't you?

Derek shook his head. "I haven't the foggiest."

It was your mind, husband. Your crazy, baffling, wonderful mind. How about you use that mind to figure out a way out of here and get our daughter back?

Officer Reynolds yawned. The lousy police station coffee wasn't doing the trick. His shift had started at dawn, and already he'd fielded dozens of calls from concerned citizens asking if the bees were still a danger, if the chief was doing something about it, and if, like the internet was telling them, it was some sort of political plot to distract from some other political plot.

The phone rang again, and he let it. Instead of answering, he got up from his desk. Might as well see how the prisoner was doing. Under the circumstances, Chief Cross had insisted they release everyone under lock and key save for the lone man stewing in the holding cell. Reynolds wondered what the guy must have done to incur Cross's wrath, but he hadn't asked. If Cross wanted the man to stay put, the man stayed put.

Walking down the hall, he stopped at the water fountain and took a drink, trying to rid his mouth of the sour taste of the coffee. Then, he opened the heavy door leading into the bank of holding cells.

When he came to the one occupied cell, his mouth fell open. Hanging from the bars was the inmate. The man's tongue protruded, as well as his eyes. He'd taken off his shirt and used it as a makeshift noose.

To say that the chief would be cross was an understatement.

"Sir?" Reynolds shouted. "Sir?!?"

The officer quickly unlocked the cell door and stepped inside. Grabbing the man around the waist, he lifted the dead weight with a grunt. Reynolds winced—he'd been on desk duty for more than a month now, ever since he'd had his appendix taken out. Hoisting a full-grown man did his belly no favors.

The man coughed loudly, startling Reynolds.

"That's it, sir. Come on back."

The inmate did more than that. He reached up, gave the shirt/noose a quick flick of his fingers, and dropped to the floor.

"Sorry," the man said. "Little bit of magic I picked up in college."

For his next trick, the prisoner looped a shirt sleeve around Reynolds's outstretched hands, tying him up like a calf. A swift do-si-do later, the officer was inside the cell and the inmate was out.

Reynolds was too flustered to say anything other than, "No!"

"I'm afraid so," the man replied. "Could you maybe tell me where I could find a shirt, Officer?"

None of the early morning crew even glanced Derek's way as he slipped past them in a borrowed police cap and fleece jacket. The officers in the bullpen were too busy answering the barrage of phone calls.

He walked as quickly as he dared down the hall and toward the doors to the outside world. He'd almost made it away scot-free, when one of the doors swung open, and a figure with a badge practically bowled him over.

"Derek?"

Shelby looked as shocked to see him as he was happy to see her.

"Did you find Mel?"

Shelby ushered Derek out of the building and down the steps to the street before answering. "She's safe. Justine finally got through to Mr. Armbrister's wife. Turns out her husband is quite the Luddite—he insists on zero technology during his camping trips. No phones, no iPads, no—"

"She's safe?" Derek felt a weight the size of Pikes Peak lift from his chest. "Where did they go?"

"Seems Armbrister is also a bit of a rule-breaker. His wife said he planned on taking the kids out to Thunder Canyon."

The weight crashed back down.

"Did you say Thunder Canyon?"

"Yes. Why?"

Derek grabbed Shelby by the shoulders. "Take me back to the Odditorium."

"Derek, what's the matter—"

"Now!"

THIRTY-TWO

"Out of the way!" Shelby shouted at the beer delivery truck hogging the lane. She sounded the cruiser's siren, and the truck lurched right, letting her squeeze past.

Derek sat shotgun, castigating himself for offering up Thunder Canyon to Mix as an option. Maybe the Texan would come up with his own plan, he thought, but he knew that was wishful thinking. Mix's team and the bees were on a collision course with his sweet girl, and all because he hadn't kept his big mouth shut.

Shelby reached for the radio once again. She had been attempting to contact Chief Cross ever since they left downtown behind in her rearview mirror, but all her efforts had been in vain. "Dispatch," the radio squawked.

"Rita?"

"That you again, Shel?"

"Yup. And I'm going to keep checking in until you find the chief!"

"If the man's gone silent, there's nothing I can do—"

"Bullshit, Rita!" Derek had never seen this side of his sister-in-law. Sure, he'd seen her steamed, but never on the verge of losing it completely. "I don't care if you have to go outside and send up a smoke signal, I need the chief to call me back."

"Hold on, Shel..." There was a commotion on the other end, and Rita returned. "He just walked in. And he is *pissed*."

"Well, so am I. Put him on."

"Remember," Derek said, worried that in Shelby's current state of mind, she might do more damage than good, "you get more flies with honey than—"

"Shut up, Derek."

"I'm just saying."

The radio buzzed, and Cross's stern voice bellowed out of the speakers. "Officer Parker, you get your ass back here to the station."

"Negative, Chief. No can do."

"Is Stratton with you? Seems he's eloped again."

"He is, but that's not important—"

"Like hell, it isn't. I need you in my office in the next fifteen minutes, or you can turn in your gun and shield."

Shelby looked over to Derek. She tilted her head the same way Molly had done when she was about to do something rash.

"Like I said, no can do."

"Sorry to hear that. *Ex*-Officer Parker."

Derek grabbed the radio away from Shelby. "Chief, listen up."

"I will not."

"Mix is planning to draw the swarm into Thunder Canyon—"

"Get off this line—"

"My daughter is in Thunder Canyon, Cross. She's there, along with a bunch of other kids. If you don't call him off, if something happens to my girl..."

The radio was silent, and for a moment, Derek thought they'd lost the signal.

"How many juveniles are we talking about?"

"Half a dozen at least," Shelby directed toward the mic.

"Shit."

"What's wrong?"

"The bird's already left the nest. Let me see what I can do."

Once more, the radio went quiet.

"You think he believes us?" Derek asked.

"We'll see," Shelby replied.

The cruiser had reached the edge of the city limits. Another ten minutes on back roads, and they'd be pulling up to the Odditorium.

"Sorry about your badge," Derek said.

"I was due for a change anyway."

Cross popped back up on the radio. "Either Mix is out of range, or he's got no interest in taking my call."

"Then, we're going to go get her ourselves," Derek stated.

"You do that, Stratton, and you're going to find yourself—"

Shelby switched off the radio.

"Shelby?" Derek noticed that she had become suddenly and surprisingly calm.

"Yup. Definitely time for a change."

She hit the gas, and soon the cruiser's speedometer was pushing triple digits.

Back at the Odditorium, Shelby remained behind in the cruiser, calling up colleagues, trying to enlist them for help behind Cross's back.

Derek stormed the workshop with a vengeance. The Tornado Suit lay in pieces at his feet. It was time for an upgrade.

He rummaged through bins of spare parts, lit up an acetylene torch, and got to work.

"Don't worry, honey. I got this."

I know you do.

After a few modifications—and a couple of nasty burns from the torch—Derek's project was complete. He allowed himself a moment to reflect upon what he'd created. Or recreated.

"I hope to God it works."

It will.

With no room for error, he slipped on his revamped suit, making sure all was in working order. And when he stomped out of the Odditorium and into the sun, looking for all the world like something out of a Marvel film, he couldn't help but feel that Molly was right. It was going to work.

Thick metal mesh had been soldered across the face of the helmet, and extra-heavy-duty gloves adorned the reinforced sleeves. Derek had removed all cameras and anything else that might weigh him down.

He was no longer Derek, the Tornado Chaser but Sir Derek the Bold.

Looking good, hon.

"Thanks," he said, removing the helmet. "Now, let's go get our daughter."

THIRTY-THREE

After throwing up for the third time, Mayor Guffey was wondering if she should have taken Chief Cross's warning to heart. The man was right—flying in a helicopter was the Devil's business. At least, that's what her stomach told her.

Mix sat across from her, waving his big Stetson hat in front of his face. Either the man was overheated or her sick was getting the best of him.

"Sorry about that," she said, dabbing at the corners of her mouth with her shirt sleeve.

"Happens to the best of them," Mix assured her. But the fact he didn't make eye contact told her that she was an outlier when it came to helicopter hurling.

Mr. Gale sat next to Mix, his eyes locked on a tablet. He wore headphones to communicate with the pilot, and gave constant updates on the swarm's location. "Thirty degrees west, please."

The mayor peered out the window. The Colorado land-scape rushed by like it was in a hurry to get somewhere, making her gorge rise yet again. She had to get her mind off the motion of the copter, and so she launched unbidden into conversation.

"We've lost about twenty hikers in Thunder Canyon over the past decade alone. We finally had to ask for it to be shut down. Shame, really. It's a beautiful stretch of...of..."

"Give me your hand," Mix said.

"Excuse me?"

Mix scooted forward on his seat and took the mayor's hand in his. He then proceeded to apply pressure to her wrist. Remarkably, her stomach cramps eased.

"Little trick a boat captain taught me in Scotland."

"What were you doing in Scotland?" Mayor Guffey's eyes were closed—she was relishing her nausea's retreat.

"Procuring some of the finest footage of the Loch Ness Monster ever taken, that's all."

"Fascinating. Tell me more." She couldn't care less about Mix's exploits, but the man's hands were working wonders. Best to let him pontificate if it meant relief from her sour stomach.

"Thank you!" Gale squealed, hand to his headphones. He turned to Mix. "The pilot's got a visual on the swarm. We're about three miles out and closing."

Mix let go of the mayor's hand. "Tell him to flank left and then head straight for the mouth of the canyon. That should let us lay down a solid trail of the atomized flowers for them to follow. Got it?"

"Yes, sir," Gale replied, relaying the order to the pilot.

Mayor Guffey—having regained her sea legs...or air legs, as it were—waved over one of Mix's camera operators. The folks with the cameras had been filming since before they took off, and by the time the adventure was over, Mix should have enough footage to fill months of programming.

"Get some shots of me, will you?" she barked at the woman with the Canon. The camera operator obliged.

"Press is power, ain't it?" Mix noted.

"You have no idea." The mayor waved the woman with the camera off. "You explained how you're getting the bees into the canyon. Once you've got them cornered, how are you going to..." She made a slicing motion across her throat.

"You wanna field that one, Mr. Gale?"

Mr. Gale most certainly *did* want to field that one. He lowered his mic and shouted, "We're going to deploy a supercharged version of Dipterex with a methomyl chaser. We've got twin canisters mounted on each side." To illustrate his point, he made the flight attendant motion, usually meant to indicate where the exits are.

"And that'll do the trick?" the mayor asked.

"If it doesn't, nothing will."

It wasn't quite the answer Mayor Guffey had hoped for, but it would have to do.

The helicopter tilted left, the pilot acting on Mix's orders. The mayor's chair, which had been lashed to the interior wall by bungee cords, strained toward the center of the cabin. Her stomach reminded her never to take a spin in a copter again.

"Here we go, folks!" the Texan hollered. "Let's make history."

The cameras turned his way.

"Damn it, you're all too slow on the draw. Let's try that again." Mix shook out his hands and grinned widely. "You got me in frame?"

"Yes, sir," the camera operators said in unison.

"Here we go, folks!" Mix repeated. "Let's make history!" He drew out "history" this time, accentuating his Texas drawl.

As the helicopter leveled out and made straight for the canyon, Mayor Guffey peeked out the window.

The swarm rose up behind the helicopter on its right side —a dark cloud rising like the hand of God. *Or the Devil.*

Mix raised his Stetson and called to Gale, "Let's lure them in!"

Mr. Gale repeated the order to the pilot, and Mayor Guffey felt a shift in the vehicle's inner workings. The helicopter let loose a white cloud of mist from its underbelly a moment later, releasing the aerosolized flower mixture directly in the swarm's path.

Would the bees take the bait? If they didn't, the mayor thought, they could pin another failure on her administration, and that would be that. Maybe she could get a job selling cars for her cousin in Loveland...

The swarm turned as one, like a giant manta ray in the sky. Whatever Mix had sprayed into the air, the bees were keen to take a whiff. As the helicopter approached the canyon, reminding Mayor Guffey of the Death Star run in *Star Wars*, the bees followed, eager to get to the source of the sweet scent.

"We've hooked them!" Mix hooted.

Even Jefferson Gale let out a triumphant whoop.

Mix looked at Mayor Guffey with a sly smile. "Maybe *now's* a good time to talk about my fee."

Mel stood poised over a longhorn beetle, net in hand and mason jar at the ready. The insect clung to a sunbaked log, its long antennae flicking as if it were trying to pick up a radio signal.

She raised her net slowly, a hunter preparing to bag her prize. But just before she could scoop up the beetle, a low chopping sound overhead distracted her, and she flinched. The insect sensed her movement and scurried for safety.

"Dang!" Mel shouted, and looked to the sky for the offending interloper.

Something large and moving fast was heading up the canyon. A white stream poured from its underside, making it look as if...

"That helicopter is peeing!" Sean McNally howled.

It *was* a helicopter. Not the little kind that took tourists around the Rockies but the large type that always showed up when there were wildfires. Was there a fire? Were they all trapped here in Thunder Canyon with flames racing their way?

The helicopter zoomed high overhead, and as it did so, the morning sun caught the liquid it dropped, forming a shimmering rainbow.

I wish I had my phone. That would make a great photo.

What came next made her wish doubly hard for her phone, for following on the helicopter's heels was a swirling, ominous cloud.

As the beating blades of the helicopter retreated, the buzzing hum of the approaching cloud rose.

Mel dropped her net.

"What is that?" Sean asked, pointing.

"Bees," Mel whispered.

The rainbow melted as the liquid fell. A droplet landed on Mel's nose, and she felt an odd numbness spread across her skin. Whatever the helicopter dropped was caustic—best to shield herself from its effects.

"Don't breathe it!" she shouted at the rest of the group, pulling the bandana around her neck up over her mouth.

Amazingly, the boys listened to her, each one in turn covering up. The only person who *didn't* listen was Mr. Armbrister.

"Would you look at that?" the man said, hands out to catch the "rain." Then, he giggled. "Rain, rain, go away. Come again another day."

"Mr. A!" Mel cried, waving frantically. "Cover up!"

"It's raining, it's pouring!" Was Mr. Armbrister catching the liquid on his tongue? "The old man is snoring!"

The bees were closing in. And there was nowhere to take shelter save for their tents. The tents would have to do.

"Get in your tents!"

"What?" Calvin Briggs asked.

"The tents! The tents!" Mel shouted.

The boys scurried for cover like mice. Mel did likewise. The only one who remained was Mr. A, who was licking the liquid off the palms of his hands. He then raised both arms over his head as if praising the swarm's approach.

"Wheeee!" Mr. Armbrister crooned.

Mel quickly zipped her tent shut.

Mom? Dad? Help!

THIRTY-FOUR

The sheet of plexiglass that served as a stand-in for the *Lightning Bug*'s windshield vibrated furiously as Derek sped down the country road, tailing Shelby in her cruiser.

"Roadblock in one mile," Shelby's voice sounded from his phone.

"I owe Sgt. Baker a lifetime membership at the Odditorium for tipping us off," Derek replied.

"He was happy to do it. He and Cross have had their own little cold war going on for the past decade. Watch it—big pothole coming up."

Her warning came a moment too late. The VW hit the hole head on and with such force, its right wheels threatened to rip loose. The Tornado Suit—lashed to the Beetle's back—jostled wildly but hung on. Derek spun the wheel to the left, righted his trajectory, and resumed his trek.

Stay calm.

"Is that all the advice you've got?"

Stay hydrated?

"Very funny."

His invisible copilot had been putting in her two cents ever since they left the Odditorium. In fact, it was Molly that sparked the idea to swing past Tom Buckaroo's farm before making a run for Thunder Canyon. Shelby had objected to the detour, but Derek insisted. He didn't dare tell her that her dead sister had insisted upon a deviation from the plan.

The Beetle gasped like a horse begging for water.

"One last trip, old girl," he promised the VW.

"What's that?" Shelby asked over the open line.

"Nothing. I think I see flashing lights up ahead. Are you ready?"

"I am if you are."

"Let's do this."

Derek cut left, taking the car off road, the Tornado Suit rattling atop like the space shuttle hitching a ride on a jumbo jet. This had to work. It just *had* to.

It's showtime.

"Damn straight, honey."

Officer Payton sipped lukewarm chai tea from his thermos. He shifted in his seat—his was one of the older cruisers in the police fleet, and as such, was built more for speed than for comfort. A couple of weeks ago, he'd participated in a charity bicycle race up in Victor, Colorado—a small mining town almost two miles in elevation—and had come home with sore glutes. Sitting watch for anyone attempting to enter the canyon should have been an easy assignment, but the combo of aching muscles and a sunken seat made for a miserable morning.

Ah, well, he thought, downing another mouthful of tepid tea.

Movement to his left caught his eye, and he stiffened like a watchdog suddenly on point. A lone vehicle was approaching, and from its silhouette, he identified it as one of his own. The chief had personally instructed him to keep an eye out for two possible gatecrashers: the kook who ran the Odditorium and Officer Shelby Parker. From the looks of it, it was the latter who was approaching.

Payton cracked his neck and stepped from his vehicle. Hands upraised, he waved down the approaching cruiser. The cruiser slowed and drew up alongside.

"I was wondering when you might try crashing the party," Payton said as Officer Parker rolled down her window. "How about we keep this simple? You turn your vehicle around, and let me get back to my chai."

"How can you drink that stuff, Payton?" Shelby asked. "It tastes like spiced milk."

"Beats the shakes coffee gives me."

Shelby looked longingly at the entrance to the canyon. "No way you can look the other way?"

"I'm afraid not."

"Need I remind you who started the FundYou account to help your sister after her husband skipped out on her?"

"Need I remind *you* that you're in unlawful possession of a cruiser, former Officer Parker?"

Shelby groaned. "Oh, come on, Payton."

"I always liked you, Shelby. But if I let you in, I might as well start looking for a job at Value-Mart."

"I've got an idea. How about we—"

"Hold up," Payton snapped, hair bristling on the back of his neck. "What's that?"

"Where?" Shelby looked around.

"Three o'clock!"

Being an avid hunter of prairie dogs, Payton was highly attuned to movement in his periphery. But what he spotted was no prairie dog. In fact, its freakish appearance was unlike anything he had ever seen before.

"What is that?" Shelby cried.

"That's what I asked you!"

"I don't have a clue."

"Shit. It's coming this way."

So it was. As it neared, Officer Payton could make out the thing's hunched spine, boney like the hogbacks that lined the foothills. And were those spikes sticking up from between its vertebrae?

Officer Parker exited her vehicle and dashed over to his side. Together, they watched as the creature approached, rasping like an engine that wouldn't turn over.

"Holy crap," Payton said. "If I didn't know better, I'd say that was a freaking Chupacabra."

"Whatever it is, it's not scared of us one bit. Damn, do you think it could be rabid?"

Payton pulled his weapon. "I'm not waiting around to find out."

He fired. The creature dodged right. He fired again. The thing dodged left, and kept on coming. He could see its glittering eyes and its shining teeth. Payton imagined those teeth sinking into his neck and fired again.

This time, his round found its mark. The creature's head exploded like a piñata, bits of fluff and metal filling the air.

What the...?

The "beast" came skidding to a halt. It tipped over on its side, revealing a set of spinning wheels beneath.

I've been had.

A loud popping noise filled the air, followed by a second. Payton sensed his cruiser sinking lower to the ground. He'd been around long enough to know a bursting tire when he heard one.

He turned to face his cruiser in time to spy a VW Beetle zipping away from the scene, something that looked oddly like the Tin Man from *The Wizard of Oz* attached to its back. Derek Stratton, no doubt—the owner of that damned Odditorium.

"Enjoy your chai," Shelby called over to him.

Distracted by the departure of the VW, Payton hadn't noticed Shelby getting back into her cruiser. The two vehicles sped off together, heading for Thunder Canyon like they were racing to beat the Devil.

Officer Payton examined his rear tires. Both were as flat as pancakes, slashed, no doubt, by that damned Stratton. He took a sip of his chai, grimaced, and poured the remainder out on the ground, watching the earth soak it up, and wondered how much Value-Mart paid its security guards.

THIRTY-FIVE

When Mayor Guffey confirmed the bees were following their trail, she gave a silent victory cheer. Dire scenarios flew from her head like bees themselves, and she allowed herself to believe that they might actually pull off this cockamamie plan.

That was until she saw the children.

"The canyon is supposed to be deserted," she said to herself but loud enough for all to hear. The dire scenarios returned with a vengeance, and the mayor knew her time in office was about to come to an abrupt end. *Mayor Incites Insidious Insects!*

"What's that you say?" Mix was out of his safety belt and out of his seat, pressing his nose to the window.

"We have to abort," Mayor Guffey replied.

"Not a chance!"

"She's right," Mr. Gale chimed in. "We can't release the poison."

"It's just glorified Raid, ain't it?" Mix fumed. "What kid hasn't accidentally breathed in a little Raid?"

"Sir!" Gale admonished.

Mix turned to the mayor. "You're gonna have to make the call, Madam Mayor. Either you're fine with a handful of young'uns coughing for a few days or—"

Mayor Guffey cut him off. "If you think I'm going let you drop poison on a bunch of innocent children, you've got another think coming, Mr. Mix!"

"Oh, shit." It was Gale. The egghead's face was as white as an egg.

"What's got you rattled, Mr. Gale?" Mix asked.

"What kind of fuel does this whirlybird take?"

"High octane aviation fuel," Mix said. "Why?"

Mr. Gale tried to rise, realized he was still belted in, and slumped back down. "Octane fuel produces CO_2. Bees zero in on CO_2."

The information hit Mayor Guffey like a lightning bolt. "Tell the pilot to get us out of here."

Mix waved her off. "I think everybody should just calm down."

"Do it! Now."

Mel huddled in her tent, hunkered down on her knees and wishing she was anywhere else. The swarm was closing in. She could hear the many tones that made up their chorus—a high whizzing noise mixed with an unimaginably low hum and, in the middle, the ever-present *buzz*.

Mr. Armbrister had not taken shelter. As she had heard her father say, Mr. A was three sheets to the wind. The mist dropping from the sky had had a profound effect on him. He was still out there standing in harm's way, crooning his fool head off.

"Oh, the buzzin' of the bees in the cigarette trees. And the soda water fountain!"

Mel closed her eyes. Whatever was going to happen was going to happen soon. The sound of the swarm was growing terribly loud. She clapped her hands over her ears and picked up where Mr. Armbrister had left off, shouting to block out the din.

"Where the lemonade springs and the bluebird sings in that Big Rock Candy Mountain!"

Something struck the tent.

Mel opened her eyes. She saw nothing at first, but then a shadow slowly crept up the side of the nylon tent. There was no mistaking what it was, but the size of it made her wish she'd kept her eyes shut. It was almost double the size of the bee she'd found on her trip to the fissure with her father and aunt. It growled like a lawnmower, and she could see the pointed tips of its feet piercing the material.

She realized two things at the same time: if it got inside the tent, she was a goner; if she left the tent, she was a goner. She was, as she had also heard her father say, between a rock and a hard place.

One of the boys in the nearby tents screamed. More cries followed. Something about knowing that she wasn't the only one in jeopardy got her to her feet. Mel's fear melted away, replaced by white hot anger.

She hauled off and kicked the bee through the nylon. It felt like punting a football. The bee's shadow disappeared, only to return a split second later. The giant insect was incensed. How *dare* she! It stung the side of the tent. When

Mel caught a glimpse of the massive stinger jabbing through the cloth, she instantly regretted riling it up.

"Git!" she shouted as she would at a barking dog. "Go! Shoo!"

Amazingly, her words did the trick. Either that or something else had incurred its ire. The bee rose upward, abandoning the girl in the tent.

Mel listened hard. She could still hear Mr. A going on and on about the Big Rock Candy Mountain, but the roar of the swarm was subsiding.

Did she dare take a peek outside to confirm her suspicion?

She did. She was, after all, her parents' child.

Mel lay on her back and cautiously opened the tent door, slowly working the zipper from bottom to top until she had just enough room to poke her head outside.

What she saw blew her mind.

The bees were rising up, twisting and turning en masse, imitating the funnel clouds her father was always chasing. The swarm's movements were willful and deliberate, and Mel strained to see what might be drawing them higher and higher.

Then she saw the helicopter that Sean McNally had so crudely said was peeing. So did the bees—they'd locked on to the trail of mist exiting the aircraft's belly and zoomed upward.

When Mel was only six, her folks took her to a small raceway near Windsor. Even at her young age, she had an excellent sense of which cars were going to outpace the others, so much so that she and her mother had placed a couple of small side wagers involving ice cream.

She'd eaten a *lot* of ice cream that night.

That keen sense kicked in once more as she watched the helicopter attempt to exit the canyon before the bees caught up with it.

The helicopter was going to lose. She was sure of it.

Still, she urged it on.

"Go faster, please, go faster."

It was no use. The black cloud of insects engulfed the helicopter. She saw a flash. A few seconds later, a loud *bang* rang through the canyon. And then, the helicopter was spinning out of control, dropping back down to earth.

THIRTY-SIX

The locked gate at the mouth of Thunder Canyon proved no match for a Fort Womack police cruiser traveling at ramming speed.

"I got this," was all Shelby said over Derek's phone as she made her run.

The cruiser struck hard and fast, ripping the gate from its hinges and flipping it into the air. Derek, who was right on her heels, had to swerve to avoid it.

"How long is this canyon?" he asked.

"About two miles. Is that hunk of junk you're driving going to make it that far?"

"Don't listen to her," Derek said, sweet-talking the *Lightning Bug*.

"Are you talking to your car?"

"You worry about you."

Derek saw the car ahead of him bounce wildly. The gravel road leading into Thunder Canyon had been neglected for years. Over time, it had deteriorated to the point where it could barely even be called a road. Large rocks jutted upward, creating a treacherous obstacle course. He'd have to keep his eyes locked on the vehicle ahead of him to help negotiate the way.

Please hurry, honey.

Molly's voice came in so loud and clear that for a second, Derek was about to reply to Shelby, thinking she had spoken.

"I'm going as fast as I can."

"What's that?" Shelby asked over the phone.

Are you really?

Derek considered this. He'd been following Shelby's cruiser since they made it past the roadblock, and his sister-in-law was, even under these circumstances, a conservative driver.

Time to let go of the reins, and get Mel back, safe and sound.

He floored it. Perhaps realizing that this would be its final run, the Beetle dug down deep and gave him an extra burst of power, like an old dog getting its second wind.

The VW veered off the road, passing a surprised Shelby on its right.

"Derek? What are you trying to prove?"

"Just following my gut."

"What does your gut tell you about those fallen trees dead ahead?"

Derek pressed harder on the gas—the Beetle's rotting floorboard groaned, threatening to give way. The increased velocity was minimal, but it was just enough to pass the cruiser and slip back onto the road before colliding with the pile of dead trees.

Shelby was *not* impressed. "Pull another stunt like that and—"

The call dropped out. They were deep inside Thunder Canyon where cell service went to die. Hopefully that was all that would be dying this day. Except for the bees. Every last freakin' one of them.

Derek caught sight of the end of the canyon—the wide gap ended in a sort of cul-de-sac. If Mel and the others had come here to camp, that's where they'd be.

He also spotted the swarm.

See? I told you to hurry.

The bees hovered high overhead, looping through the air like an enormous comma. And swirling about them was a cloud of rising smoke. What had happened here?

A quick scan of the scene ahead gave Derek his answer. Mix's helicopter, his pride and joy, lay in a heap atop a dozen downed pine trees, crushed under the weight of the falling aircraft. Black smoke poured out of the top of the copter, and what remained of the blades spun fitfully. If there were anyone alive inside, it would be a miracle.

As he drew closer to the headwall of the canyon, he spied a man standing alone near a cluster of bright, neon tents. It had to be Mr. Armbrister, the man who'd whisked his daughter into this mess. He was going to have words with the man, oh yes, he was. But as he pulled up next to Mr. Armbrister, Derek had a strong suspicion that the fellow was in no condition to discuss anything.

Mr. Armbrister had stripped down to his boxer shorts and was busy covering himself in dirt.

The man was high as a kite.

"Down came a honeybee and stung him on the nose," the stoned man yowled. "Little Robin Redbreast fell down and tore his clothes!"

Derek jumped out of the Beetle, and, ignoring the loopy gentleman, made for the tents.

"Mel! Melissa! It's Dad!"

"Dad?" came a small voice from inside one of the tents.

"Mel?"

Derek's daughter cautiously emerged. When she saw her father, she rushed to him and threw her arms about him.

"I'm sorry," Mel said, her voice halting. "I...I..."

"I know, sweetie," Derek replied. "It's all right. Don't worry, I'm here."

"Little Robin Redbreast sat upon a tree—"

"Pipe down, will you?" Derek hadn't noticed Shelby pulling up behind him. Now she was busy trying to get Mr. Armbrister to put his clothes back on.

Mel grabbed her father's face. "Dad, the bees are here. There are millions of them. They smashed a helicopter!"

The distant pop of something exploding in the wreckage yanked Derek back to the gravity of the situation. If Mix and company were off the playing field, that meant that he was it. Hopefully there was still some bee ammo left in Mix's copter to be salvaged.

"Get the kids in the cruiser," Derek directed Shelby.

"How many are there?" Shelby asked.

Mel counted on her fingers. "There's Bobby and Sean and...and..."

"How many?"

"Five boys, me, and Mr. A."

A rumble from above caught their attention, and they looked up. Derek's mouth went dry as he saw the mass of massive insects rotating above their heads, looking as foreboding as the arrival of Gozer the Gozerian or the aliens from

Independence Day. He'd always sought out the odd and unusual—if he survived this, maybe he'd settle for a bit more of the routine and familiar.

"Just do it. And do *not*, under any circumstances, try to drive these kids out of the canyon."

"Cars, CO_2, bees. Way ahead of you." Shelby nodded at Mr. Armbrister, who was stripping again. "What about him?"

"Stick him in the trunk," Derek suggested.

He glanced over at the site of the crash. Was that someone waving their way? There was only one way to find out.

Derek looked into Mel's eyes and said, "You keep those silly boys calm, you hear?"

"Yes, Dad."

"Team Stratton?"

"Team Stratton."

With that, he kissed his daughter on the top of her head and made a mad dash for the crumpled copter.

THIRTY-SEVEN

The closer Derek got, the worse the accident appeared. The helicopter's shattered blades were barely spinning at this point. Spilled fuel and sparks from the torn fuselage ignited isolated grass fires about the copter. Derek knew it was only a matter of time before the flames reached the fuel tanks. He had to move quickly.

The first person he spotted—possibly the one he'd seen from across the canyon—was a disoriented man in a charred linen suit. The bee attack and subsequent crash had left Jefferson Gale in shock. He stumbled about on the rocky ground, as distracted as Mr. Armbrister was. His shoes were nowhere to be seen.

Derek had no time to coddle the man—he grabbed Gale's shoulders and shook until the fellow locked eyes with him.

"How many people in the helicopter?"

"I think we crashed..."

"You, Mix, the pilot...how many more?"

A pudgy hand rose from the wreckage, waving a singed Stetson. "That'd be a lucky seven, Mr. Stratton."

"Mix?"

"In the seared flesh." Big Jim Mix rose up from the remains of his copter. The man looked like he'd tangled with a grizzly bear. "Unfortunately, the pilot and co-pilot have gone to that big round-up in the sky. But the camera folks are still kicking. As for the mayor—"

"The mayor's with you?" Derek thought he must have heard wrong.

"You still with us, Madam Mayor?" Mix asked.

"Get these damn bungee cords off my chair!" came a voice from behind Mix.

"Yup, she's still with us."

"We...we crashed!" Gale slipped away from Derek as the reality of the situation flooded over him.

"You need to get out of there," Derek warned. "This thing could blow any minute."

Mix held his hands up. "The shutterbugs and I can manage the mayor. What *you* need to do is salvage the canister fastened behind the left front wheel."

"What is it?"

"A sling to fell Goliath."

"Sorry, I don't—"

"Poison, Stratton. *Bug* poison. Take it and use it on the bastards." Mix caught his balance.

"You sure you're going to be all right?"

Before Mix could respond, Gale screamed.

Derek whirled about in time to see the unlucky man covered in bees. He'd seen TV shows where people let hundreds of the things crawl over their face and neck, growing a "bee beard." It only took a few of these monsters to cover the same acreage.

Derek's eyes shot up. The cloud was descending, and some of the more industrious of the colony had broken free from the group, opting to scout out their next point of attack.

Unfortunately for Gale, *he* was that next point.

"Mommy! Mother, oh, Mommy!" Gale wailed as more bees joined the others. Some latched hold of his clothing, others plunged dagger-sharp stingers into his flesh.

He was still screaming when they took to the sky, dragging the entomologist with them.

Derek stared after the doomed man in stunned silence. Gale's demise was so similar to Molly's that, for a moment, he found himself frozen in place.

"Snap out of it, Stratton!" Mix cried.

Derek did just that. He scrambled to the wreckage. The scent of melting plastic was overwhelming. He spied the mayor, still trapped in the cabin trying to chew her way through a bungee cord. The look she gave seemed to say, *What the hell are you looking at?*

He located the canister still lashed to the bottom of the copter. It was dented but seemed intact. He wrenched his arm trying to wrestle it free, and white-hot pain shot through his injured bicep.

Plenty of time to worry about that later, dear.

"Thanks for nothing, honey."

Derek held out the canister in front of him for confirmation. Mix gave him an exaggerated nod.

"That's it!" Mix shouted at him, batting away a bee. "Now, git."

"And do what, exactly?!?"

The Texan offered up a pained grin. "Go make history."

THIRTY-EIGHT

Mel was the last kid into the cruiser. She'd thought her father was joking about putting Mr. A in the trunk, but apparently, Aunt Shelby didn't think so. Their camping guide was safely tucked away with the spare tire and road flares. He had returned to singing about the Big Rock Candy Mountain but was forgetting most of the lyrics. By the time she crawled into the front seat along with her aunt and Calvin, he'd abandoned the words completely and was giving a terrible rendition of a trumpet solo.

"Dad will be back soon," she told Shelby, willing it to be true.

"Of course he will." But Aunt Shelby sounded less than convinced.

Calvin began bawling. She didn't really want to put her arm around him, but she knew tears were contagious. Dad expected her to keep the boys calm.

"Don't worry," she said, employing the same tone she'd heard people use with their whimpering dogs. "Everything's going to be okay."

The VW sitting beside the cruiser backfired, scaring everyone—even Shelby jumped. Mel abandoned Calvin, scrambling over her aunt to get a look at what was going on.

She caught a fleeting glimpse of her father behind the wheel. He didn't wave to her or acknowledge her in any way. His eyes were fixed dead ahead.

The *Lightning Bug* lurched forward, kicking up rocks. And then it spun about, tearing off the way it had come, leaving a dust storm in its wake.

"He's leaving."

Aunt Shelby looked back at the boys squished together in the back seat. "I know you're uncomfortable, but I need you boys to stay away from the windows."

Mel grabbed Shelby's arm.

"He's *leaving!*"

"Mel, I need you to help me," Shelby said.

"What?"

"Are you listening? I need your help."

"With what?" Part of her knew that her aunt was just trying to distract her, but another part really wanted the distraction.

"What kind of story do you think these boys would like?"

Mel thought about it and felt the tiniest of laughs rise from inside. "Something about farts."

"Really..."

"Yeah, watch." Mel put her mouth up against her forearm and blew. The resulting raspberry caught the boys' attention, and they instantly went silent, waiting for more. She obliged. Raspberry number two made her audience burst into laughter.

A bee landed on the cruiser's hood. It glared at her as if it held a personal grudge.

Its body possessed a metallic sheen, while amidst the plates adorning its torso, a collection of black and yellow hairs sprouted. It looked like a bee going into battle.

Aunt Shelby switched the cruiser into accessory mode and pressed the windshield wiper fluid button. The resultant stream was directed toward the window, not the bee, but its sudden appearance seemed to do the trick. The oversized insect took to the air.

"So," Shelby said, launching into the story. "This is the tale of Little Tommy Toot." She nodded at Mel to provide the sound effect.

"Pp-ff-t-ff-ppp!" Mel's imitation of a post-burrito stinker was spot on. The boys roared with laughter. *Bees? What bees? Ha ha ha!*

"Now, Tommy had a terrible time when it came to his toots."

Even Mel laughed after her own "musical" accompaniment.

Another bee landed on the cruiser, this time on the back window. Sean McNally screamed.

"One day when Tommy was at school—"

Henry Swink screamed, followed by Bobby and Miguel. Calvin was the only boy not screaming, and Mel suspected it was because he was peeing his pants.

"I said," Shelby continued, "one day when Tommy—"

A second bee landed on the back window. Another crawled up the passenger side window. Soon, a whole raft of insects crawled across the vehicle—so many that they blocked out the sun.

Mel looked at Shelby. Her aunt needed to keep the story going, otherwise, hysteria would take over.

There was a reason Shelby was silent. She was one of the bravest women Mel had ever known. She was a cop, for goodness sake. But she learned that day that even adults, even adults who are *cops,* have their limits.

Shelby was frozen stiff with terror.

Mel glanced around the car. The boys were out of their minds with fear, and Shelby was out to lunch.

She was on her own.

One of the tires blew, followed by the others, stung, no doubt by the ever-growing gathering of bees. The cruiser vibrated with the swarm's collective hum.

Everything is going to be all right, she told herself.

The bees proved her wrong by cracking first one window and then another.

The creatures wanted in.

Mel was afraid they were about to get their way.

THIRTY-NINE

Derek gripped the wheel tightly as he raced back toward the entrance to the canyon. He felt awful; he felt like he was abandoning his girl. But he only had one plan left in his arsenal, and it meant putting as much distance between himself and the others as possible.

Don't beat yourself up. You always do that.

"That's easy for you to say," Derek answered. "You're just a voice in my head."

Is that really all I am to you?

The VW hit a rut in the road, and something broke free from the vehicle's belly. Maybe it was the muffler or an exhaust pipe—either way, the *Lightning Bug* was now growling like an angry bear. Sound or no sound, it kept on speeding forward, giving Derek every ounce of juice it had left.

"Why are you so chatty all of a sudden?"

Do you want me to be quiet?

He didn't. Derek knew what he had to do, and it scared him to death. And while he might be speaking to nothing more than a figment of his own overgrown imagination, it still comforted him having Molly—even a manufactured version of her—at his side.

"I'd never tell you to be quiet. We both know how *that* would go over."

Are you trying to say I talk too much?

"No, I'm trying *not* to say that."

Careful, husband.

The canyon mouth lay up ahead. One last burst of speed, and Derek flew past the mangled gate and out onto the plains.

Clear of Thunder Canyon, he veered right. The slope up to the cliffs overlooking the chasm was steep, but he didn't have time to worry about that now. The Beetle would either make it or it wouldn't. With all the heart he'd put into the car —the miles of replaced wiring and the warehouse of replaced tires—his gut told him that the little car could do it. But what if his gut was wrong?

I think the time for "what ifs" is past, don't you?

He did. Derek gunned it, and the *Lightning Bug* began its climb. By the time he reached the top of the hill, steam was rolling out of the car's backside. He never understood why German engineers had chosen to put the VW's engine in the rear, but now he was glad for it.

Having finished his ascent, he sped off along the canyon's upper rim, retracing his initial trip to the interior. The drop-off to his right was a good one hundred feet, but he tried not to think about it. He had enough on his plate.

Would you like me to sing to you?

Derek snorted. It was one of their old jokes. Molly couldn't carry a tune to save her life.

"I think I have enough working against me, thank you very much."

Babe! How rude.

God, he missed her.

About a mile in the distance lay a large promontory dotted with pines. Perhaps some secret spring made the unlikely spot a haven for trees. In any case, once he reached that point, his odometer said he should be directly above Mel's campsite.

"You know, there might be another reason why you're coming in so loud and clear, my dear."

Oh? And what might that be?

"Maybe I can hear you so well because we'll be together soon."

There was no response from the ether.

"Oh, come on. I said 'maybe.'"

The sun, which had been playing peek-a-boo with the clouds, broke through, painting the promontory yellow and gold.

Derek finally eased off the gas. The *Lightning Bug* shuddered and began to slow. Its final ride was at an end.

"Thank you, girl," Derek said, patting the steering wheel. Then, for clarity's sake, "I was talking to the car, not you."

Still, Molly remained silent.

Maybe that was for the best. He didn't need anything to distract him from what came next.

He got out of the car. The heavy scent of overflowing coolant was heavy in the air, and the VW hissed like a balloon leaking air.

Derek walked cautiously to the edge of the cliff and

looked down. At first, he didn't know what he was seeing. When it came to him, his hands shook.

The campsite, the tents, the cruiser...they were all blanketed in a sea of black. The swarm had descended, engulfing everyone he cherished. He could only imagine what Mel and Shelby were going through, how terrified they must be.

Less thinking, more doing.

Derek detached the revamped Tornado Suit from the Beetle's back and laid it out on the ground. There was no way he'd be able to perform the next steps while trapped inside the bulky outfit. Best to have it at the ready so he could slip into it quickly.

Derek went back to the VW and pulled Mix's canister from the back seat. The Texan's tank of poison was fitted with a brass valve. When he'd wrestled the canister free of the mechanism for deploying its payload remotely, the valve had bent awkwardly. He only hoped that, when the time came, he could get it to work.

He set the canister next to the suit, opened the passenger side door, and eased out the item that had been riding shotgun since his detour to Tom Buckaroo's farm: a keg of mead with Tom's modified shower wand attached. The busty woman in the bee costume smiled at him as he moved the metal barrel into place at the canyon's edge. Having seen how much the bees had enjoyed Tom's product, he figured it might make effective bait.

That's when it struck him—he didn't know if the old fellow was still alive or not.

Would Tom's bachelor party novelty do the trick? He prayed it would.

With the skill of a seasoned partygoer, he began pumping. The amber mead came in a trickle at first, then a gush. Derek pumped away furiously. Liquid shot out of the showerhead in a golden spray.

"Here goes nothing, honey."

With that, he pointed the wand out over the edge. A helpful breeze caught the mead, dispersing it before letting it drop precipitously into the canyon.

The first part of his plan was working. He could taste the sweet mead in the air. Would the bees taste it as well?

They have to, he thought. They just have to.

The world outside the cruiser's windows had turned yellow and black as the swarm completely covered the vehicle. The cruiser rocked under the weight of the bees. They couldn't turn them over, could they?

The boys were freaking out, and who could blame them? It was like something out of a zombie movie, but instead of the living dead trying to get into the car, it was buzzing bees. The sound of their legs on the glass was enough to drive anyone mad, and unless Mel could distract the boys, that's exactly what would happen to them.

"And then...!" she cried, trying to drown out the droning swarm. "The king of the land, King Fartface the Third, told all of his people that no one in the kingdom could fart but him."

As a whole, the boys remained terrified, but she'd caught Bobby Lamar's attention. He'd stopped screaming and was staring at her with a perplexed look on his face.

"That's right! No one could fart but the king. And so,

everyone walked around not farting. They didn't fart in the morning; they didn't fart in the afternoon—"

"They didn't fart at night," Bobby added.

"Correct! And after one week of zero farts, what do you think happened?"

The cruiser shuddered as the bees shifted to a higher degree of fury. Aunt Shelby blinked, coming out of her stupor.

"What...what was that you said?"

Mel waved her arms in exaggerated frustration. If she'd yanked Shelby back from the brink of terror, she could reel in the boys as well.

"I said, 'After one week of no farting, what do you think happened?'"

Miguel raised his hand as if in class. "They couldn't help it and they farted?"

"Yes!" Mel shouted, giving Miguel a high five. "The whole kingdom let out the biggest, loudest, smelliest fart that the world has ever—"

A new wave of bees slammed against the passenger side of the cruiser. The vehicle tipped up on its left wheels, balanced there briefly, terrifyingly, before it dropped upside down on its roof.

Glass shattered. The angry insects tried to wedge themselves inside. The boys howled in fear, and Aunt Shelby pulled her pistol.

The swarm whirled about the vehicle—they were forming a funnel and the police cruiser was at its center. Was this what her mother had experienced before being sucked up into the tornado?

The cruiser shuddered as it lifted off the ground, drawn

up into the raging vortex of the bee tornado. It was over. Mel clamped her eyes shut. There was nothing left to do but scream.

The vehicle was airborne for a few seconds when it suddenly, and quite forcefully, crashed back down to earth. Its passengers were shaken but otherwise uninjured.

"They're leaving!" Miguel cried.

Mel opened her eyes. Miguel was right. The bees were retreating. She spied sunlight peeking through the broken windows as the bees took to the air, abandoning the cruiser.

Soon there wasn't a single bee to be seen.

Mel had no way of knowing for sure, but in her heart, she knew who had drawn away the bees.

Dad!

Derek felt the bees' approach before he saw them. A warm rush of air, sweetened by Tom Buckaroo's mead, wafted up from the chasm below. If he'd had any doubts about the effectiveness of the fermented beverage, they were gone. It was a shame old Tom wasn't there to see how Derek was putting his prized mead to use.

He chanced a look over the canyon's edge, and any self-congratulatory thoughts he had went up in smoke.

The swarm roared upward, flying parallel to the canyon wall, coming straight for him like a runaway freight train. An unstoppable force with no immovable object to keep it in check.

He would have to become the immovable object.

"Shit!" he cried, admonishing himself. He wasn't going

to do anything standing here in the open. He needed to get into the Tornado Suit. He needed to get prepared.

Derek turned so quickly that he stumbled over Mix's canister. Catching his balance, he raced to put on the suit before the bees' arrival. But the suit had other plans. Some of the welds he had made—which were initially pliable—were now set and tough as steel. It made getting into it all that more difficult. The suit wasn't the easiest to put on, wear, or maneuver—it was only meant to withstand tornadic winds. Now, with the clock ticking and the swarm almost upon him, wriggling into it was a nightmare.

He was still struggling to put on the last glove when the vanguard of the relentless swarm shot up past him, zooming skyward. The fact that they didn't try to take him out immediately meant he had a couple of seconds to grab the canister and solidify his stance.

Derek bent down—no mean feat in the suit—and made a grab for the tank. Weighed down by his metal-clad outfit, he misjudged and, instead of clutching the canister, knocked it out of reach and sent it rolling toward the cliff's edge.

The ground leading away from him sloped downward, and the canister kept going and going like that damned Energizer bunny.

There was nothing else to do but leap for it.

Derek took several clanking steps toward the escaping cylinder before launching himself after it. He felt like a bronze statue toppling over. He hit the ground hard, the fall knocking the wind out of him. But there was no time to recover. He had to stop the rolling canister before it plummeted into the canyon.

His hand found the tank a second before it disappeared

over the edge. He held on tight, dragging it back to him and clutching it to his metal breastplate.

"That was almost the ballgame right there," he coughed, trying to regain his breath.

Derek rolled on his side. The swarm continued to pour into the sky, each wave of bees adding to its ranks. He felt like he was looking up into a black hole—a celestial body eager to devour him.

He quickly ran his hands along the tank, feeling for the valve as bending his neck was impossible with the metal guard encircling it. As he lay there, helpless save for the metal cylinder he held in his shaking hands, he wondered how he'd gotten here, sprawled at the edge of Thunder Canyon with the sky overhead teeming with gargantuan insects that should have perished with the dinosaurs.

Guess you're just in the right place at the right time.

The return of Molly's voice buoyed him, and he forced himself to sit up.

"Where have you been, wife?"

I wasn't too keen on all that talk about seeing me soon.

"Really?" Derek asked, struggling to his feet. "You really think your guy is going to make it through this in one piece?"

One piece? I never said that.

With every phrase, the voice in his head sounded more and more like Molly. If his wife, with her joyous sarcasm and needling ways, had been physically present, the words out of her mouth would have been a match to those he was now hearing.

"Thanks for the vote of confidence," Derek said, raising the canister like a soldier readying to fire a grenade launcher.

Derek?

"Yes, honey?"

This is going to be bad. It's going to be very, very bad.

"Okay..."

But Derek?

"Yes?"

Molly's voice faltered, and in that fleeting moment of hesitation, the bees swooped down with ruthless determination. No words could adequately describe the sight—the swarm's descent resembled the approach of death itself.

I love you.

Derek felt fear fall from him like scales. He twisted the valve, and a fine mist shot forth.

"I love you, too."

And with that, the bees attacked.

FORTY

When Derek was eighteen, a U-Haul van collided with his little Geo Metro. He was driving to Denver to take in a retro horror film festival when a van traveling north veered into his lane and struck him head-on. The cops and the EMS workers said it was a miracle he survived the crash with only a broken collarbone. The driver of the van had vaulted through the windshield and lay *behind* Derek's car. To say the man was dead would be an understatement.

Derek hadn't remembered the other vehicle striking his —the shock of the impact must have short-circuited his memory. But it all flooded back to him as the bees plowed into him, knocking him to the ground. Their assault was epic. It felt like a giant was pummeling him with bowling balls.

He'd already used up one miracle; was there any chance there was one more with his name on it?

Make your own miracle, babe.

She was right. As always.

The poison hit home, driving the already raging bees into

a terrifying fury. They tried to burrow into his suit at the seams and stabbed at the metal armor with their icepick-like stingers. The weight of them was incredible. Insects had always seemed such ethereal creatures, riding on the wind like dandelion fluff. But there was more lion than dandelion to these buzzing monstrosities.

Then, true to its name, the bee tornado began to form. Derek felt gravity ease as the suction caused by the rotating swarm tried to lift him off his feet. Another few seconds, and he'd be dragged up into the heavens.

He frantically aimed the canister all about as if torching the things with a flamethrower. The poison was damn effective. Bees that got a direct dose dropped immediately, falling to the ground where they writhed in agony. Those that received a glancing spritz found themselves instantly disabled—flying about in haphazard circles. Some tried to find safety in numbers, attempting to reform the tornado structure. But all they managed were a couple of lopsided twisters resembling clumsy whirling dervishes.

The ground at his feet was littered with the bodies of the dead and dying. Still, the swarm pressed forward. One bee managed to insinuate its stinger into the seam at his neck. While it didn't pierced his flesh, it scratched him deep enough that he felt a hot rash spread quickly across his throat. Oxygen began escaping from the helmet. Derek tried shouting and found that his vocal cords had gone numb. He had held his fear in check up to this point, but the loss of his voice scared the hell out of him. What was next? Would his throat close up? Would he asphyxiate?

Hush, husband. How about I do the talking, and you do the killing?

It sounded like a good bargain.

As Derek sprayed the swarm in wide arcs, he noticed that when a poisoned bee collided with another, the second bee promptly succumbed to the same fate as its counterpart. The bees were spreading the toxin to each other.

The bees were dropping like flies, yet still they came, undeterred by the metal man with the canister. The scene reminded Derek of a vintage video game he used to play— Galaga, the one where you shot pixelated bugs from outer space. He was, by anybody's estimation, racking up quite the high score.

Don't get cocky.

If he still had use of his voice, he would have said, "I thought you married me *because* I was cocky." Instead, he blasted away at the next wave.

He felt the stream from the end of the cylinder grow weaker. Taking a quick assessment, he figured if the canister could hold out for two minutes more, there wouldn't be enough bees left to pollinate a garden. And a small one, at that.

The spray hesitated, caught a second wind, and finally sputtered to halt. Mix's special mixture was no more.

Derek dropped to his knees amidst the pile of twitching bees. The poison that had felled the insects burned his lungs. Add to that the ever-increasing swelling of his throat, and he knew his bee-killing was at an end.

The few buzzing behemoths that remained airborne weren't long for this world. Some performed kamikaze runs against the rocks, exploding into green and yellow goo. Others tried to escape to a higher elevation, only to find they didn't have the strength to do so. They too crash-landed in gory fashion.

A single bee crawled toward him over the twisted corpses of its fellow hive-mates. Derek knew the multifaceted eyes trained on him were connected to a primitive mind. Still, he couldn't help but feel waves of hatred coming off the creature as it approached.

Derek raised the canister, waited for the bee to get right in front of him, and brought the cylinder down. The resultant *crunch* reminded him of cracking open boiled crabs with a mallet.

He dropped the tank. No more. The end.

He unlatched the helmet and removed it, taking in big gasping gulps of air. The poison, still wafting about, made him wretch, but it felt good to be free of the headgear.

Honey...

"Not now," he croaked, working to remove his gloves.

You know that in Galaga, after you clear the board, there's an extra challenge?

"Yeah?" Where was she going with this?

Well...

Whether her voice had conjured the low rumble he now heard or it was the other way around didn't matter. What mattered was that something was coming up behind him. Slowly and deliberately.

Something *big*.

Derek turned and faced his extra challenge.

"Oh, God..."

A bee was rising up from the canyon. One last bee to test him, to challenge him. But *this* was no regular bee. It dwarfed its companions. In fact, it was as large as a grizzly bear.

"The queen."

Tom had spoken of such a creature. She was the reason the others were so protective. How protective would *she* be, seeing that he had massacred her swarm?

Her face was dotted with hundreds of eyes, each one glassy and gleaming in the sun. A wild thatch of antennae sprouted from her head, and her wings hummed like a high voltage transformer about to blow.

Derek was outmatched and out of ammunition.

The queen dipped her enormous torso, showing him her massive stinger. He never knew if queen bees possessed stingers, but now he had his answer. Hers was aimed straight for his heart.

Derek?

"Yes, Molly?"

For Mel?

Derek's eyes welled up with tears.

"For Mel."

The queen readied to strike, but Derek struck first. He rose to his feet and ran for the bee. His legs had nothing left to give, and yet somehow, miraculously, they gave just a little bit more. The queen seemed to sense something was off, and backed away, hovering over the chasm.

No matter, Derek thought. Ready or not, here I come.

With all the grace of a knight in shining armor, he leaped over the cliff's edge, hands outstretched.

Derek's fingertips felt the queen's furry flank, but there was nothing to grab hold of. His hands quickly slid down the bee's side until his right hand grasped the barbed length of one of the queen's rear legs.

The two dropped into Thunder Canyon.

They spun as they fell—the queen trying desperately to stay aloft as Derek tried desperately to hang on. Down and down they went, their fates locked. And as Derek noticed the ground rushing up toward him, Molly gave him one last bit of advice.

Let go.

Who was he to argue?

He let go of the queen's leg and crashed into the top of a pine grove, hitting every branch on the way down, each impact slowing his fall ever so slightly.

When Derek hit the ground, he felt bones snap like kindling. Unconsciousness rushed toward him like a missile, but before he blacked out completely, he caught one last glimpse of the queen.

The bee writhed some thirty feet above him, impaled on one of the pines he had snapped on his way down.

Derek would have liked to confirm she was dead, but the darkness had other plans. As he slipped into oblivion, he felt Molly's arms about him and heard her gently singing in his ear.

Out of tune.

He smiled and let go.

FORTY-ONE

The aspens forming the perimeter of the Mount Bennett Cemetery had been inching their way toward the fall for a few weeks. With the days getting shorter, the trees' leaves were now a vibrant gold. A breeze came down from the Rockies, causing the leaves to flutter, making the aspens appear as if they were adorned with butterflies.

Derek stood before Molly's grave. He'd been too numb with grief to give the headstone much thought when the funeral director had walked him through the burial process, but he had to admit that the stone, cut in the shape of the hogbacks that lined Fort Womack, served its purpose well.

His name and year of birth were chiseled there as well. The only thing missing was the date of his demise. Derek breathed deep. *That date*, Derek thought, *could wait.*

He knelt before the grave, struggling to do so with the pin in his knee. His collarbone was barking as well—the old break from his youth hadn't endured his fall from the cliff. There were other breaks—ribs, toes, and a slight pelvic fracture—and there'd be other hospital visits as well. But he was in one piece.

Really? Because I heard Dr. Early say that when you arrived, you were in about fifteen or sixteen pieces.

"I can't get anything by you, can I?" His voice was still rough, and the specialist he'd seen was uncertain when or if it would get any better. Derek had never lit up a single cigarette in his life, but his new voice made him sound like a lifetime smoker.

Big day.

"It is."

Then why are you haunting my grave?

Derek didn't speak directly, mainly because he didn't know the answer. But when he did, he found the truth in his words.

"I needed to say thank you."

What for?

"Just...thank you, that's all."

Don't you get maudlin on me.

Derek grinned. "Too late."

He knelt there awhile, enjoying the crisp air, herald to the season's change.

When he finally rose, not without much effort and pain, he felt a shift. Whether it was in the wind or in himself, he wasn't certain, but he was suddenly certain that his time of hearing Molly so clearly was drawing to a close. She'd been there when he needed her, but now it was time to head back to the Odditorium and get started with the rest of his life.

"It's not going to be the same without you. Ever."

I should hope not.

"Any words of wisdom from the great beyond before I trundle on home?"

Don't forget who you are.

"And who might that be?"

Molly laughed, and the aspens shuddered in the wind, their leaves laughing with her.

Why, Sir Derek the Bold, of course.

He bypassed the main road to the Odditorium, opting instead for the dirt trail leading to the back of the building. The used Fiat he'd picked up in Greeley got him here and there, but it wasn't, and never would be the *Lightning Bug.*

Before slipping inside the living quarters, Derek peeked around the corner at the parking lot. It was packed, and cars were still coming. Good thing he'd hired a couple of extra parking attendants.

Funny, the old Derek—the Derek with full use of his vocal range—would have been counting heads in cars and coming up with a rough calculation of the day's take.

"It's just nice to see the parking lot full again," he said, surprising himself.

He opened the back door and stepped into the living space. Shelby and Justine were making the world's largest salad while Mel got familiar with her new phone. People had been so generous—they'd set up half a dozen funds to get him back on his feet. And the gifts! New phones, fresh produce, ten years of internet completely free. Even Big Jim Mix had pitched in, offering Derek a ten percent cut on all the footage his team had taken on what had been commonly called B-Day.

Mel saw him first, and leaped up to hug him. He'd told her over and over to go easy with her embraces, but it was no use. He heard his bones creak as she squeezed him hard.

"I have something for you!" she squeaked.

"For me? What, like a present?"

"Yeah!"

She tossed aside her phone—a miracle in and of itself—and grabbed a flat, rectangular package from the kitchen table. Shelby and Justine shared a look, and he knew that they had had a hand in it.

"Open it, open it!" Mel cried, handing him the package.

Derek slowly, carefully began to peel the gift wrapping from the box.

"Oh, come on!" Mel complained. She grabbed the package, tore off the wrapping for him, and handed him the slim box.

Inside was a tie. Derek was *not* a tie guy, but *this* tie?

"I love it."

"Really?"

He held the tie up for Shelby to see. She smiled. "You need help tying that?"

"I think it might come back to me."

After a few misguided attempts, Derek managed to knot the tie. He turned to the mirror to examine himself.

The pattern was a honeycomb. And here and there, small honeybees flew about, busy at their tasks.

"Are you ready?" Shelby asked him.

"Let's do this."

The city had erected a temporary stage for the event, complete with bright purple and white bunting. The press was in attendance, gathering sound bites, snapshots, and video to plaster all over social media and send to the national networks.

Canned music had the crowd dancing, and foam beehive hats appeared to be all the rage.

The crowd spotted Derek and his family and roared, drowning out the mayor, who was well into her introductory speech. The din was overwhelming, and Mayor Guffey thought, to hell with it, and threw focus to Derek.

The reception was overwhelming. It wasn't every day that one got to save their hometown, but it wasn't like he'd done it alone.

Tom Buckaroo was in attendance with a custom black and yellow-striped artificial arm. If the dynamite he'd used to try to stop the bees had had a bit longer fuse, he wouldn't be sporting a prosthesis. At least, the old fellow was still alive and kicking. Tom had his new arm around a new lady friend, and the smile on his face said that he was going to be just fine.

Big Jim Mix, Shelby, Justine, the late Jefferson Gale... everyone had played their part. Heck, it took an entire cast to bring *Hamlet* to life—the Melancholy Dane couldn't tell the tale on his own.

"Thank you," he said into the microphone standing center stage. "Thank you all."

The applause kept coming. He raised a hand and urged them to stop.

"I think it's important to acknowledge Mayor Guffey's leadership during this time of trial." They were Shelby's words coming out of his mouth. She'd told him putting in a good word about the mayor would go a long way to mending some bridges. "In fact, it was her idea to turn next year's event into the ShakesBee Festival!" The idea had been Derek's, but he allowed the crowd to cheer Mayor Guffey. The mayor favored him with a nod.

"Tom Buckaroo? I'll forever be in your debt."

"Just pay me for the mead you stole, Stratton," Tom called, eliciting peals of laughter.

"I'd like to welcome back to the world Hercules Adams and Benny Shale, two brave young men who tangled with the bees and have lived to tell the tale." He leaned into the mic conspiratorially. "You members of the press might want to chat them up."

Herc and Benny waved to the crowd. Benny seemed no worse for his run-in with the insects. He'd simply woken up after about a month in the hospital and started asking questions about why he was there. Herc, on the other hand, would bear the scars of his encounter for the rest of his days. He stood supported by a walker. His skin was awash in healed wounds—pale, raised lumps marking every sting. Still, he raised a fist in defiance, and the crowd rewarded him by chanting, "Hercules, Hercules, Hercules!"

"Finally, I'd like to thank my sister Shelby and her girl-friend Justine for going above and beyond. If there are any car dealers in the audience, I owe Justine a new Outback."

Mel shifted at his side, seemingly nervous he was going to forget about her.

"I think that's it...oh, hold on! Where's my head?" Derek turned to Mel and held out his hand. "The Odditorium's Grand Reopening wouldn't be complete without thanking someone who not only represents the best of her mother and me, but is one of the bravest young women I know. Melissa? Would you do the honors?"

Mel motioned him to bend, and she placed a big kiss on his cheek.

"You ready?" he asked.

"Yes!" she said.

The two of them walked over to the large object at the stage right side of the platform. It was covered with a gold sheet. Mel took hold of one of the corners. A canned drumroll sounded from the speakers.

"One...two..." Derek said.

"Three!" Mel shouted as she yanked the sheet free.

A collective gasp rose from the crowd followed by thunderous applause. The queen bee, expertly mounted on a large steel spike, impaled in perpetuity, stared out at the audience with her myriad eyes. No kid had ever come back from one of Mr. Armbrister's bug hunts with a specimen so grand.

"Citizens of Fort Womack," Derek shouted. "The Odditorium is open for business!"

ACKNOWLEDGMENTS

Enormous thanks to my family, Mom, Steve, Pete and Kristin, gave me the time to lure these bees into the light. A tip o' the hat to my wonderful band of beta readers: Mark Aldrich, Leslie Farrell, Steph Hilliard, JoAnne Sorensen, Kristin Sorensen, Steve Sorensen, Steve Stred, and Nick Sullivan. Thanks to Gretchen Douglas for her proofing prowess. And much love to my wife, Deborah Graybill, for helping me pursue this crazy craft.

ABOUT THE AUTHOR

Chris Sorensen is the bestselling author of *The Nightmare Room, The Hungry Ones, The Messy Man, Suckerville* and *Bee Tornado*. He's penned over a dozen plays for Thin Air Theatre Company and the Butte Theater of Colorado, including *A Haunting at the Old Homestead, The Vampire of Cripple Creek,* and *Dr. Jekyll's Medicine Show*. He lives with his wife and pups in the Garden State of New Jersey, where he splits his time between writing spooky stories and narrating audiobooks. Chris has narrated over 250 titles for Audible Studios, Tantor Media, Recorded Books, and many others. He is a member of SAG-AFTRA and the Horror Writers Association. When he's not writing or recording, you can find him haunting old bookstores and Indian restaurants.

ALSO BY CHRIS SORENSEN

Suckerville

The Nightmare Room

The Hungry Ones

The Messy Man

and

The Mad Scientists of New Jersey